Passable *In* PINK

The Novelization

Novelization by
E.L. LESSERT

Adapted from the Screenplay by
JERROYLD HOLT

SUNSHINE BEAM PUBLISHING

SUNSHINE BEAM PUBLISHING

Sunshine Beam Books are published by
Sunshine Beam Publishing, Inc., Hollywood, CA 90072

Design by Anna Huff

First Printing, June 1983
Second Printing, September 1983
Third Printing, November 1983
Fourth and fifth printing, March 1984

PRINTED IN THE U.S.A.

Addy placed her copy of What Color Are Your Parachute Pants? *down. She grabbed a seat within the cubicle that held the library's computer. She watched in absolute shock and fascination as the giant green screen began to display random and strange shapes: circles, squares, lines.*

What exactly was happening here?

And then this popped up:

"Hey ADDY? You around?"

Huh? Was someone communicating with her—or trying to—through the computer?!

She typed:

CMON GRIMER. STOP TEASING.

Not knowing what else to do, she then hit RETURN. Could this possibly *work?*

Addy stood and peered over the cubicle at the other students. No one looked her way.

It was the Desolate Land of Shhhhhh.

Sitting back down, Addy noticed that the screen was now displaying the following:

WHOS GRIMER?!

Addy gasped. If it wasn't Grimer ... it just had to be Roland. *But how was he talking to her via the computer?*

"HOW ARE OU DOING THIS!" typed Addy, in such a rush that she forgot to type the 'y'.

Addy erased everything she'd just written and retyped the sentence.

It was now correct.

She did not like mistakes.

Again, not knowing what else to press, she touched RETURN.

She waited.

Before Addy realized what was happening, and as if in a dream, stick figures of a boy and a girl appeared on screen, a short distance away from each other, and then closer, until finally they were holding hands.

Addy secretly prayed that these two computer characters would kiss.

But they quickly did much more. Addy became ill...

Credits

Director ....JERROYLD HOLT
Screenwriter ....JERROYLD HOLT
Producer ....MARK ERIKSON BENARAY
Kristina Sheffer ....ELKI
Addy Stevenson ....ABIGAIL GORDEN
Roland McDough ....MICHAEL WIRTZ
The Grimer ....JUSTIN WOOD
Student Who Discovers
Severed Ear But Ignores It ....SHANNON LINDER
Student Bit by Friendly, Rabid Goat.....................BUZZY NECO
Student Fast Asleep in Sex Ed ....JIMMY TOEM
Student Wearing Pleated Leather Gym Shorts ... AMELIE CANCO
Student Who Owns Two
"Ghetto Blasters" ....DAPHNE ELISABETH
Student with Non-Clicking TV Remote ....AMER YAQUB
Student Who Gives Speech
That Wraps Up All the Themes..................ELAINE ZELDA LEVIN
Lone Female Playing
"Cards with the Male 'Tards"...........................LUCIANNA ELLIE
Heterosexual Student Listening to
"Jesus Christ Superstar" in Red Grand Am ....MIKE S.
Student Seen in Last Freeze Frame .... MARK LARNICK
Student Playing Yello's "Oh Yeah"
at Top Volume..GERALD LEON
Student Diddling with Himself
in Handicapped Stall ....ELLIOT KORTMANN
Student, Bullish and Tough and
Fully on Purpose.. GORDON CARTER
Student Crouching Over Toilet Seat
Like Prehistoric Bird ....SUZANNE ROSEN
Hoots the Owl..HOOPS THE OWL
The Gooch.. TED TRAVELSTEAD
Clearasil Rep ....JENNI K.
Gorgeous Sweetheart ....KATIE I.
Photographer of ET poster............................ MADHURI SHUKLA
Leering Endodontist...JACK JACKS
Teacher Incapacitated by "Kentucky Flu" ....SKITCH LYNCH

Credits

Music...MARK ROZZO
Lyrics..STEVE WILSON
On-Set Photographer...SETH OLENICK
Stylist ....PETER BALTRA
Designer ....ANNA HUFF

The filmmakers wish to thank the town and citizens of Shermer,
Illinois, as well as Yvonne Mendard, Monk Vintage, Shermer
High, Jack Pollock for illustrations, Tim Barnes for riding a bicy-
cle with a space creature, Mayor Mary Jane Byrd for "Greasing
the Wheels"and Sunset Diner for"Greasing Those Tummies!"

Foreword

Jerroyld Holt was a recluse who wrote and directed four movies between 1981 and 1984: *Twice Around the Moon, The Original Six, Ghost in You,* and *Passable in Pink.*

By most accounts—what few exist—he was a strange man. Born in 1953 in Holland, Michigan, hard east by the shore of Lake Michigan, Hoyt had aspirations to become a filmmaker from a very early age, ambitions put on hold after his draft number was unceremoniously plucked from out of the proverbial steel helmet in a June 1971 lottery and his presence immediately requested at Parris Island as a Marine recruit.

Stories about Hoyt and his strangeness have echoed down through the years from those who (tenuously) knew and worked with him—anecdotes about his reclusive nature, his peculiar eating habits (he insisted on using two knives and *never* a fork), his practice of not looking anyone directly in the eye. Perhaps his eighteen months "in country" accounted for these oddities, although it's hard to imagine anyone suffering from PTSD after doing hard time in an air conditioned Saigon press office.

Most likely, Hoyt was *always* a bit off, thinking differently from his classmates and later his fellow Marines, spin-cycling his way through off-beat ideas that he hoped to one day turn into movie scripts and then, eventually, into feature length films.

We might never know. Although Hoyt worked with hundreds of actors and crew members over the course of his short career, he never did consider any of these co-workers to be a friend.

By the same token, no one ever claimed to be his.

Because there are no surviving interviews available with Hoyt, and he passed away in 2006, he's oftentimes referred to as the "Kubrick of Teen Movies," but that might not be entirely accurate. Hoyt's cinematic work was always warmer than Kubrick's, always filled to the brim with raw human emotions and a more upbeat worldview on what we're all capable of, no matter the age.

If you've never seen a Hoyt film—and if you didn't at the time, in the 1980s, you probably won't be able to now, as they're nearly impossible to find—you're truly missing out on some of the most influential films from that era.

Hoyt's influence is ever present in today's pop-culture landscape: cinematic teens who listen on-screen to the very same alternative songs they'd actually listen to in *real* life; a filmmatic world in which teens can not only say *fuck* but actually *do* it; an understanding of what it means to be a father, a mother, a teacher, all of one's hopes and dreams in the rearview, just struggling to get through a "typical" day.

The power of these movies upon the few who saw them in the '80s cannot be overstated. It's similar to the apocryphal story of the twenty or so people who purchased the first Velvet Underground LP in 1967 and then went on to start their own (much more) financially

Passable In PINK

A Prom-Com

CHAPTER ONE

Arrival!

The house was in an uproar, and—as was typically the case—Addy Stevenson was already seeking shelter in her pink-cocooned nest of a bedroom, just above the garage where her parents parked their twin blue Volvos, the dork mobiles she liked to call "Tweedledweeb" and "Tweedledumb," but only when her parents weren't around to hear.

As stupid as the cars looked—and as embarrassed as Addy was to be seen chauffeured around in them— she still needed the wrecks (not to mention her parents) to get practically anywhere, at least until she acquired her license in exactly eight months, three days and three hours.

Not that she was counting.

In the meantime, Addy was stuck like a caged bird inside of her own house with her spastic spaz of a younger brother and her golden princess of an older sister, both super annoying, both more spoiled and more deserving—*clearly*—of all the attention that their parents could ever afford to dole out.

Addy on the other hand—until the day she died— would remain smack dab in the middle, like the keystone in a stone archway: *entirely useless and utterly ignored.*

There was a large crash outside her bedroom. Only 8:30 A.M. on a Saturday morning and already there was chaos.

And then the inevitable bark of her father: "Addy! *Open*! We need to get moving! Now!"

Addy was standing in front of her "Wall of Fame" that was covered from floor to ceiling with black and white magazine clippings of half-naked, hairless, non-threatening white boys in their tightest of tight underbriefs, as well as large colorful posters of homo-sexual lead singers of little-known British alternative bands.

Clearly, this was a typical teen girl's room!

Staring at her own reflection before her full-length mirror, Addy wasn't liking what she was seeing, which was of little surprise. She often didn't. Hips too wide. Breasts too small. Nipples mulberry-shaped. One reminded Addy of an inverted nuclear button she had seen in the movie *The China Syndrome*. She spent at least an hour a day gently drawing it out.

Addy was no fan of her body. She could have used a lot more encouragement about it. Not that anyone, besides Addy, had seen much of it recently, although there had been that one boy on the church trip in eighth grade who had come awfully close while they played "Seven Minutes in Heaven" in a McDonald's bathroom while on their way to Six Flags.

The boy had sobbed and passed out.

He now worked part-time in the remote-controlled-car aisle of a Radio Shack on the outskirts of town.

More banging and another crash. And another bark

2

from her father:

"Addy, I said *now*! Downstairs! We're all meeting in five!" he emasculated.

"I said I would be *there*!" cried Addy, even though she hadn't. No matter. "*Geez*!"

Let 'em wait, she thought. *It's more important that I look good.*

Addy couldn't control all that much about her life but she could certainly control how "Ramba" she looked, which meant "rambunctious," which meant "cool." No one used the word "cool" anymore—they hadn't in a long, long time, going back to at least when her parents were teens, back when the dinosaurs roamed the Earth—and if anyone now *did* use the word "cool," guess what?

Then you were no longer "cool."

But who was Addy kidding? Only Rich Richies and the Well-Heeled Flushies and the Lake-Dwelling Casherios could ever truly be "Ramba."

Never in a million years could a girl from the scraggly northwest side of the lake—and living in a mediocre red-brick 5,000 square-foot Winnetka Georgian house with a half-circular driveway and a full three-acre backyard—ever be considered "the slip-drip tip-top from the bang-out slang-out."

But that was okay. Addy was different. She was *Tive Tive*, which meant *alternative*.

She mentally ran down her outfit, starting from the top:

Wide-brimmed men's black floppy hat on a nest of candy-apple red curls ... *check*.

Deep-dangly earrings fashioned out of wine corks,

stains still visible … *check.*

Pink satin brocade vest that came down to her knees and just beyond … *check.*

A pair of ripped and stonewashed denim jeans torn in all the *right* places, with a hand-sewn, designer brand insignia on her back-left pocket that read "**NO** BRAND!" …

No brand.

Was there anything more Tive Tive?

Finally:

An oversized black tuxedo cummerbund formerly belonging to a homeless man who lived beneath a bridge in downtown Chicago and that still smelled of sudden death … *double check!*

Was there anything more non-conformist?

Most "def" not.

Not bad, Addy thought. *Not bad at all.* Some of the other students at Northridge High, the "straights," might think of her as looking "insane" or "unhinged," but Addy truly felt that she looked as good as she could possibly look, and would even rate herself a seven. Maybe an eight.

Definitely enough to *pass* … a spunky charmer with mismatched accessories who had once torn apart her grandmother's priceless 1930s wedding dress to create a pair of kicky jazzercise leg warmers.

It was the only heirloom her grandmother had left her—or anyone. The white satin leg-warmers hadn't kept Addy at all warm—not even close—but it had so been *worth* it … Addy had been the *supreme hit* of her 7th grade disco roller-skating party!

What remained of this outfit—and it wasn't much—was now attached to a wooden stick and used to scrape down the backyard barbecue.

Addy turned away from the mirror and walked over to her bedroom door, past the life-sized male "Yarnkin" creature, the one she had fashioned the previous winter from large chunks of Styrofoam and huge reams of thriftshop fabric and thread, stepping over and around a sea of smaller creative handmade arts and crafts projects—including a nautical-style tampon holder and a sweat headband fashioned from repurposed Bazooka Joe bubble gum wrappers she prayed wouldn't dissolve when she'd experience her first sweat—and then pulled open the bedroom door with an announced flourish:

"*Behold*! The *glamour* that is Addy!"

Her younger brother, Justin the Jerko, was running down the hallway and nearly tripped over Addy's lace-up black-leather boots. He laughed sarcastically: "Watch it, *retardo*!"

"Don't you have boogers to pick somewhere?" quipped Addy. She had a fast mind.

"Yeah, right here in my nose," wisecracked Justin, flaring his nostrils. "*Eat* 'em, sis!"

"Gross!" replied Addy. "Get *broke*!"

The patter was coming fast and furious.

"C'mon, let's *go* already," interrupted their father, pushing them both aside. He was buttoning up his dress shirt and wending his way through the chaos. "The Riccardacchios are arriving any minute!"

The Riccardacchios! Great. So *that* was the source of all this hubbub!

"Don't you mean the *Retard*dios?" calloused Justin, thirteen and a freshman in the very same school Addy was attending as a sophomore.

He was smiling, of course. He was *forever* smiling.

Addy's older sister Mary Anne—otherwise known as "the princess, most fair and lovely" or just "the princess"—had announced a few days earlier that she was engaged to a certain "Anthony Riccardacchio."

The young couple had met the previous weekend when Mary Anne had impetuously decided she was hungry for ethnic food and foolishly headed south of the lake to ingest a heaping slice of deep-dish pizza topped with uneven slivers of cured pork and beef, all served by a hirsute Italian with a complicated nose who had never once so much as traveled north of the south end of the lake, and—even worse—had never had any desire to do so.

It was simple: the north side of the lake was the very best. The east side was okay. The west side, acceptable. The south side ... very much *unacceptable*. And anyone who lived within a thousand miles of Chicago, with the exclusion of those on the south side, knew about this.

It was a complicated way in which to exist, but it was the *only* way.

As for Addy and her family, they lived on the west side. The *north*west side of the west side, which was suitable. The north*east* side of the west side, on the other hand, well, that was better left to anyone stupid enough to choose to live there. Addy had never been anywhere close to this area and had zero interest in ever doing so.

Nobody in Addy's family was particularly happy

about their geographic set of circumstances but the 5,000 square-foot red-brick Winnetka Georgian house with the half-circular driveway was adequate and it would just have to do until Addy's father pulled down more money as an advertising copywriter in downtown Chicago.

Her father's latest advertising campaign for a national fast-food chain—"Where in the hell is the goddamn beef?"—had failed miserably. He was still tweaking a new slogan—working days and nights to the chagrin of his family—but he was having an extraordinarily difficult time bringing forth the vision in his head.

"Fuck is the Beef?" had also not caught afire.

And neither had "Give Me a Hamburger Already! I Am Old and Cannot Afford a More Expensive and Better-Tasting Meal!"

Advertising was difficult.

As for this current family situation, things were only looking worse.

Addy's parents, to say the least, were not overly-thrilled that their eldest daughter had decided to marry at the age of nineteen.

Not that nineteen was too young.

What bothered them more than anything was that the princess was dead-set on marrying an ethnic whose breath and body odor stank of Mediterranean herbs and unpleasant, far-off spices.

Addy came from a long line of proud WASPs, with nary a drop of seasoned blood that looked or smelled in any way that could ever be considered "global."

The Stevensons considered themselves the American norm. Especially when it came to food. With the exception of the princess and her Italian-styled pizza, the Stevenson family had consumed ethnic food only one other memorable time, back in February 1980 ... a luke-warm schnitzel platter served on a paper plate within the German section of EPCOT Centre that later caused explosive diarrhea in the Mexican section of EPCOT Centre.

That had been enough.

But say what you wanted about Addy and her family ... they were nothing if not exquisitely *gracious* hosts.

"Can I help?" asked Addy, now downstairs and in the kitchen. "Anything I can do?"

Her mother was frantically unwrapping a square package of American cheese and rearranging a fistful of Ritz crackers on an upscale plastic party tray *just so*. The cheese had the density of an imploded star.

Her mother was known for having the "touch." She had long wanted to start her own catering business that would specialize in getting buzzed and rearranging food in a way that only she could appreciate, but was so far having a difficult time coming up with the necessary funding.

If that dream never came to fruition—and it was looking more and more like it never would—she desperately wanted to open a franchise that would specialize in selling delicious cookies—preferably *gigantic* cookies—just like the ones created by her favorite celebrity millionaire chef, Famous Anus.

It was the hottest food craze! The bigger, the more scrummy!

"Yes, you can help," answered her mother, tongue

out, an intense look of concentration on her face, sipping a Bartles & Jaymes wine cooler, oh-so-carefully placing a small pyramid of Rice Krispie treats on a single sheet of dot-matrix sprocket-fed computer paper at just that *perfect* angle. "You can help by making yourself scarce."

She was wearing her brand-new lace oven mitts made so famous by Madonna in the above-ground Jacuzzi/ dance scene in *Desperately Seeking Susan*. They were fingerless, which was of little use when it came to avoiding burns, but they looked absolutely *Marv Marv*, which meant intensely marvelous.

"Let me tell you something, Addy," her mother warbled. "Even if you aim for mediocrity, life is *still* a goddamn pain in the ass."

To accentuate her point, she floated a flattened stream of menthol cigarette smoke directly to the rumored heavens above. She took another sip from her wine cooler.

Addy sighed. She'd been hearing this *bon mot* since her soul was too young to be crushed by it. And she was only trying to help her mother! *Like she even wanted to be here for this stupid event!*

Could things get any worse?

A scream came across the skylights.

They *could*.

"Ahhhhhhhhhh!!!!!!!!!!!!!!!!!!"

It was a most *terrible* sound.

It reminded Addy of the noise Coco Hernandez made after suffering that horrendous compound fracture after dancing without permission on top of a moving New York City cab in *Fame*.

And it could be originating from one—and *only*

9

one—family member ... Addy's older sister, the princess, dolled up in her most expensive fancy dress and stinking powerfully of her favorite Yves Saint Laurent perfume "Upscale Suburban Drug Store."

Addy and her sister had never particularly gotten along.

They looked so *different*!

One was blonde of hair, perfect of nose, rosy of cheeks and tall of height.

A swan.

The other: a stumpy, brooding, dinosaur-armed mess.

A runty petting-zoo duck.

To Addy, and perhaps to the rest of the world, it was very clear as to which sister was which.

Pacing back and forth, the princess now seemed to be—no surprise, this house was so *lacking* in surprises!—a nervous wreck. Dramatically putting her hands up to her head, she howled: "I *haaaaate* this stupid family! I'm so embarrassed! I want to *diiiiiie*!!!!!!!"

"You sure there isn't anything I can do to help?" Addy asked her mother, who was now busy writing a grocery list in the voice of an unreliable narrator. Addy remembered the last grocery list in which "KEEBLER MAGIC MIDDLES" had been scrawled more than three hundred times.

"Stick your head into the microwave oven and press START?" Justin impishly suggested.

There was that smile again.

Addy lunged for the twerp but missed. Justin stepped clear just in time. He bolted over to a spot just behind the "natural wood" Formica kitchen counter.

10

And then he did a strange thing.

Instead of calling Addy by any of her hundreds of nicknames, he clapped his hands together a few times as if calling over a family pet.

But the family had no pet.

Instead, an Asian teen instantly appeared by Justin's side.

"Who's *this*?" asked Addy, confused.

"This would be the Chonger," said Justin. "He's living with us for the rest of the school year."

"Since when?" asked Addy.

"Since *today*, schizo," said Justin. "C'mon, Chonger. Dance your dance!"

The Asian teen, dressed in typical American attire—a casual silk shirt beneath a pastel designer jacket, sleeves pushed all the way up to the elbows—began to shuffle back and forth, counting off dance steps in heavily accented English.

And then he screamed: *"Time to boogie for the all night fever!"*

Justin giggled even harder, which only encouraged the kid to dance that much more spastically.

"What's going on?" Addy asked her mother. "You know about all of this?"

The scene was almost like something out of a movie written by a man who never once met a real-life Asian.

"Our new transfer student from the Chinese continent," slurred her mother, now arranging paper cups on an imaginary ornate tray in a haphazard, random pattern. "We want this Chonger to experience a very nice life in a *civilized* country. And besides," she continued, "today

11

is March 1st. This has been on the calendar for months."

Addy froze. "Did you say March 1st?"

"Yes," answered her mother, slowly. "March 1st, Addy."

"March 1st," said Addy, mostly to herself. "*Unbelievable*."

"Faster, Chonger!" screamed Justin, highly amused. "Dance *faster*!"

Instead, Chonger pretended to throw and then catch an American football.

He did it all wrong.

It was pathetic. And yet Addy had to admit that this Chinese exchange student was infinitely more amusing than the East German or whatever the hell they had the previous year. He had lasted only one week before leaving to join the American Marines fighting in the Middle East. He had found the atmosphere in Beirut more relaxing.

"Just unbelievable," continued Addy, walking out of the kitchen and making her way upstairs. "*March 1st!*"

The front doorbell rang.

It was the comforting sound of a leaf blower at full throttle on a Sunday morning.

It went off again.

Addy kept climbing to the second floor. *Forget all this lunacy,* she thought. *I give up!*

Entering her room at the end of the carpeted hall, she slammed the door behind her shut. The muted greetings of her parents and the Radacchios down below could only faintly be heard.

Addy stood before her full-length mirror and talked

rectly at her own reflection.

"They forgot," she announced, sadly: "They fucking forgot! Unbelievable!"

Her reflection stared back at her, just as sad.

Perhaps even sadder.

How could this have happened?

They had forgotten!

Everyone.

Mom. Dad. Justin. Princess Mary Anne.

Even the Chonger!

True, Addy had forgotten just like the rest of them, but wasn't that what parents and siblings and newly-introduced exchange students were for? To remember so their children or siblings or host family minor dependents didn't have to?

The celebratory noises from below amped up a notch. Addy could hear snatches of conversation:

"Welcome!"

"American cheese!"

"Don't sit on the couch!"

"We thought all Italians

events?"

Addy pressed her

delicious feeling

In a weird

ing with

wi

ne
der, wi
who could
box filled with
from a world of anim
drunken adult misogyny.

The Electric Salamander sp
knacks to teenage girls and close
quite fit in with the rich "Ramba" cro
pers might have found these items to be "u
to Addy, and her ilk, they meant the world.

The store was stocked from top to bottom:

Telephones in the shapes of fruits, vegetables and yummy edibles!

Reversible buttons reading "PRUDE" on one side, "SLUT" on the other!

Anti-apartheid bumper stickers that went perfectly on the back of any Volvo or Ford Escort!

The store also sold creative, colorful posters one couldn't find anywhere else in the mall—*or perhaps anywhere else in the world!*

Addy's favorite featured an image of a flying unicorn eating waffle fries while riding a grinning dolphin beneath a Skittles-colored rainbow. A pink rabbit sat just off to the side, leisurely playing a lute, while a winged cherub danced alone, wearing a backwards Kangol hat but no pants.

"Even your parents?" Addy asked again.

CHAPTER TWO

The Grimer

"They forgot?" asked Kr...
truly forgot? Outrageous!"
Addy nodded unhapp...
She was just thankful...
feel miserable alone...
Kristina Sheff...
been since Add...
tended the...
Kris...

"*Especially* mine," responded Kristina. "They were *so* out to lunch! They totally forgot the anniversary of my first period! I had to celebrate all by my lonesome! And that's when I moved out of the house for good and became the assistant manager here at the Electric Salamander!"

Kristina lived in a small apartment next to the mall where she worked part-time after school. She was incredibly mature for her age and looked it: although she had only turned sixteen a few months ago, she appeared to be at least forty-seven.

Kristina tried to wrap herself in a tough veneer but she was as sensitive as they came, as proven by the button she wore on her overalls that read "Obviously I've Made a <u>Serious</u> Vocational Error!"

The button was extraordinarily funny.

And yet it also made the very serious point that perhaps Kristina was cut out for something much bigger and more important than selling mass-produced ironic knick-knacks to teenage girls and closeted boys who didn't fit in with the rich "Ramba" crowd.

One day, not very long from now, Kristina would become an assistant manager in the richer part of the mall, perhaps at the Purple Palsied, a store that sold only the hippest of teenage medical supplies, including black-and-white checkered scoliosis back braces in corduroy and teen catheter bags in a multitude of neon colors and enviable brand names.

For now, however, Kristina was stuck on the wrong side of the mall—in a "poor store"—far away from any of the customers with the fancy pumps and the loafers without socks who shopped for crewneck sweaters and ruffle-knitted rompers, all paid for with their daddies' American Express Platinum Cards, with "available credit" to the moon and back.

"Yeah, but I wouldn't take it too seriously," Kristina continued. "You can always celebrate on your own."

"I suppose," said Addy. "But I still don't have a boyfriend. Who am I going to celebrate with?"

"Hey!" said a teenage girl, walking into the store. "I need help over here! Like *now!*"

Kristina rolled her eyes and walked over. She had no other choice. She was a feudal laborer. The customers, the kings and queens.

"Take your time," the girl muttered sarcastically. She was holding a bag from Neiman Marcus.

Kristina walked even slower.

"Do you sell three-pack neon scrunchies?" the customer finally asked when Kristina reached her.

"No," said Kristina. "And I could have told you that from the *other* end of the store."

"Stupid Yoid," said the girl, turning to leave, but not before throwing a glance at Addy, who recognized her as Cathy Douglas, someone she used to be friendly with back in the third grade. They had stopped hanging out after Cathy had heard a rumor that Addy's mother only purchased generic Pixy Stix.

Kristina walked back over to Addy, still sitting on the counter, next to the cash register. "She comes in here once a week to ask for things she *knows* we don't have. Wish she'd just stick to the Richie area. *Whatever*. I have more important things to think about. Like

17

sucking face with Choad tonight."

Kristina was currently dating a fifty-six-year-old drummer from an all-white alternative and synth-pop band with a "Minneapolis sound" called Funk-Chanel. His name was Choad and he played the drums standing up, as all the great drummers throughout history have insisted on playing. The keyboardist for this band dressed, for whatever reason, in hospital scrubs.

Kristina was a whole lot more sexually experienced than Addy, as evidenced by her incredibly large "HUG ME! I'M NOT A VIRGIN ANYMORE!" button. Kristina had lost her virginity at the age of fourteen inside a strip-mall's tanning booth. Or so she said.

Addy had still not seen, let alone touched, her first "real-life" penis, although she *had* once observed a scrambled version on her parents' cable long after midnight. Even the condom was pleated.

"I truly could use a *real* boyfriend and not a stuffed animal or one made out of yarn," complained Addy.

"Ya got a point there, kiddo!" declared Kristina. "Twice the people, twice the *fun*!"

Addy laughed in a prudish manner. It felt good to get out of the house and "hang" in her all-time favorite place in the world, the breathtaking indoor mall, so that she could "rap" with a loyal friend who was basically the same age but who was that much more "clutch" about life. Kristina had once performed oral pleasure on a one-legged vagabond named Butchy. She later provided the play-by-play to Addy in the school cafeteria with baby carrots as props, as the entire student body watched and applauded. Addy could only shake

18

her head in wonder.

All the guys tended to adore Kristina, even if she did look to be in her fifth decade.

"That may be the case," responded Addy, sadly. "But let's admit it: I'm not one of those girls who has ever turned heads. Like *you*!"

"Well, maybe it's time you *started* turning them!" exclaimed Kristina, laughing. "Start turning those boys' heads *now*!" Kristina made a jutting motion with her own head. "Start with *this* one!"

Addy turned just in time to see a familiar face entering the store.

The Grimer.

King of the weirdos.

Total freaka-Yoid. A gimpy Twimpy fool.

A spine-spackin', wonder jackin', easy-rackin', Toughskin-sportin' senior without a single functional clippitin'-clappitin' clue …

Capable of damn near *anything* …

And here the Grimer now came, riding a unicycle, juggling two large blades and a bowling ball. The Grimer was wearing full harlequin makeup and his hair was on fire.

Anything for a laugh!

Typical Grimer.

Addy sighed.

If he wasn't so pathetic, Grimer *might* even be amusing.

Maybe.

To Addy, Grimer was little more than a goofy kid who smelled bad. Sometimes when Addy closed her eyes, Grimer's smell reminded her of that retainer she had mistakenly left in the backseat of her father's car for more than a year after she had eaten a Chicago style hot dog topped with onions, relish, sour pickle, hot and spicy yellow mustard, and about fifteen other toppings, including a handful of vinegary crinkle fries.

The Grimer poured a large cup of Orange Julius on his head, extinguishing the flame.

"Hello, ladies!" he proudly announced. "Grimer has arrived and in *style*! For it is his job to entertain!"

He unicycled in place, twice as fast, still juggling.

"You done?" Addy asked, already knowing the answer.

"Never!" said Grimer. "Just *beginning*!"

Grimer dropped both large blades, narrowly missing Addy's feet, and jumped off his unicycle, leaning it against the front counter.

"How goes it?" asked the Grimer. "Does it good go?"

Interesting: *He had just reversed the order of a clichéd greeting in order to make it sound fresher and more Ramba.*

"You're taking good American money from out of my mouth!" announced Kristina, feigning annoyance. "Customers are too scared to even enter this shop with you here!"

"You *loooooooove* it," enunciated the Grimer. "And now for a song!"

Grimer got down on his right knee in his best imitation of Al Jolson doing "Mammy."

Addy and Kristina cracked up.

The kid was funnier than Yakov Smirnoff! Perhaps

even funnier than the funniest of them *all* ... the San Diego Chicken!

Still down in the kneeling position, Grimer reached for Addy's hand. "May I have your hand in marriage?" he asked in a comical voice. "To have and to hold? To mostly hold? And if the light is right, to *kiss*?"

Addy blushed and pulled her hand away. "Never, Grimer," she said. "You know I love you as a friend ... but—"

"Always the clown, never the clownsmaid," finished Grimer, with great fanfare. He pretended to weep, which only made Kristina laugh that much harder.

"Grimer, you're about as funny as a tainted Tylenol capsule!" stated Kristina. "But I *work* for a living. And these mass-produced bespoke items aren't going to put themselves away!"

It was hilarious and everyone laughed very, very hard.

Addy stopped laughing suddenly—and no one knew why.

"Oh my dear Lord-in-Heaven-17," she unexpectedly cried.

Addy was staring longingly towards the store's front entrance.

Grimer and Kristina followed Addy's penetrating gaze.

Now they knew.

There, about five yards away, stood the most beautiful boy in all of Northridge High.

And he was a Richie....

Addy often fantasized about this very scenario in her

bedroom while dancing alone as Echo and the Bunny-men's "Bring on the Dancing Horses" warbled queasily on her pink boombox's cassette player.

It was an apt song because riding a horse was a terrific metaphor for having sex, at least for Addy, who had never had it.

She had also never ridden a horse.

Then again, horses were non-threatening when it came to a "self-pollution" visual aid.

But never in a million years—never, ever, ever ... even in the foggiest notions of possibility—did Addy think that something this glorious could actually happen in real *life!*

"Oh my Lord," exclaimed Addy, palm clutching her forehead as if she were about to faint.

"He dressed *left*," muttered Kristina, staring at his crotch.

"What does *that* mean?" Addy inquired.

"One day," Kristina said, giggling, "you'll *know*."

Addy looked forward to seeing her first real-life penis. She imagined it would look *stunning*—sleek and neat and super clean—with luscious curves, a flawless triple combination of hue, texture and warmth.

And if it didn't?

Well, *no problemo*.

She'd just accessorize it with repurposed bangles and lightly-clinking magical bells. She would improve on it with feathers and other good-luck talismans until it looked *bewitching*.

"Lord!" she announced again.

"How many times are you going to say *Lord*?"

complained Grimer, annoyed. Whether he was upset that his comedy routine hadn't earned as many laughs as he had hoped, or whether he was merely jealous that Addy was no longer paying enough attention to him, or whether the viscous peachy liquid suppurating from the third-degree burns he'd given his forehead earlier were irritating him, was not entirely clear.

What *was* clear was that Addy was in love.

He's a total buck, Addy thought dreamily. *A bohunk! That fresh-swept haircut! It must have cost $30!*

Addy was already fantasizing about calling his home phone number and coquettishly hanging up as soon as he answered …

"You've never seen Roland McDough?" asked Grimer, an edge to his voice. "As in 'McDough's got the *dough*?'"

"Leave her alone," declared Kristina. "Poor thing's shipwrecked on Planet Hormone!"

And then in a very managerial tone, Kristina announced: "You can walk into the store, you know! We're *safe*, I promise you! We won't bite." She paused. "Unless you ask *nicely*."

Roland McDough—windblown blond hair perfectly set in place, modeling loose and cool khakis, wearing a wrinkled gray linen jacket, a white shirt open at the bottom collar, and a facial tan primed while observing a Hispanic mow his exceedingly large lawn for an entire hellishly hot afternoon—grinned. It was a shy grin. A grin that if it could talk in a mid-Atlantic accent and not in a grating Chicago inflection might lock-jaw: *I do have a lot of money.*

This boy ... oh, he looked so very *crispy*.

"I'm ..." Roland started. "I'm ..."

The Grimer made a "hurry up" motion, as if to say *Hurry up!*

Addy smacked Grimer directly on his bony shoulder. He made a great show of acting hurt.

Served the idiot right!

Roland, not seeming to notice or care about the crazy antics taking place before him, continued: "I ... I've never visited this end of the mall before. It's ... certainly most *interesting*. I am here because I would love to buy a button."

"A funny, alternative button?" asked Kristina. "If that's the case, we've got whatever you need!"

Kristina pointed to a rack that contained all manners of incredibly hilarious buttons, including one that read: "Frankie Says Fuck Off."

"No, not at all," responded Roland. "A *normal* button. For a white Izod. Mine fell off. While tending to my championship mare, Whinny."

"Championship mare?" asked the Grimer. "Who in the hell owns a championship mare? Who is this zagnut?"

"Roland," answered Addy, barely paying attention. "Roland *McDough.*"

"I *know* his name," responded Grimer, annoyed. "I told *you* that."

Meanwhile, at the entrance to the store, Roland took a giant step back. He looked perplexed. He *hated* being confused.

He also hated being hated. Not from afar, necessarily,

but up close. Too messy. *Too much work.*

"Let me correct myself," cravatted Roland. "My horse is technically a castrated male. A gelding. And mine is a miniature. But I liked the name Whinny so very much. That was my grandmamma's name. She died. Of old age. And, in some sense, bullet wounds. But she wouldn't have been at the dialysis center on that fateful day if she wasn't old."

"Great story," Grimer replied sarcastically. "This guy's a real Phil Donahue."

Kristina took a small step forward, carefully, so as to not scare the puppy-like creature cowering at the store's entrance. And then, very slowly and without a sudden movement to so much as frighten a gentle Richie, she soothed: "No. This end of the mall does not have *those* types of buttons. Have you tried The Tasseled Loafer on the *other* end of the mall? It's next to the store that sells gag cassettes for outgoing messages, After the Beep for Cheap."

"I haven't, no," responded Roland. "Should I try there?"

"I would, *yes*," said Kristina, as if speaking to a three-year-old.

Roland didn't move, only sluggishly bobbed and weaved. He looked similar to a kidnap victim blinking out a distress signal in Morse code. At long last, he gave a slight smile and a limp wave. He retreated, the lingering odor of Ralph Lauren Polo's delightful "in your face and up your ass" cologne the only evidence he had ever stopped by. This, too, was only sold in the rich part of the mall, as well as the fancy atomizers that

25

dispensed it.

"*That guy*," said Grimer. "Wow. He definitely ain't the sharpest loofa in the golden shower."

"No," said Kristina. "Nor is he interesting. But he *is* single. I do know that."

"Why?" asked Addy. "How is that even *possible*?"

"How?" answered Kristina. "Because he's more dull and useless than those endless fund-raising segments that interrupted those awesome *Live Aid* musical acts!"

Addy still had her palm on her forehead. She didn't care. He was a *Richie*. And handsome. What else did a girl need?!

The fantasy she had thought about for so many years had *finally* come true and it was better than she had ever daydreamed: *A Richie shows up at the entrance to the store where her best friend assistant-manages and asks a question that makes very little sense. Richie tells a story that goes nowhere and isn't very interesting ... all the while, Addy remains all pouty and mum.*

Oh, it was *delicious*!

Long gone was Addy ever caring that her parents had forgotten the anniversary of her first period!

How silly that all seemed now!

Whooooooooosh! See ya in the rearview!

It wasn't until a few hours later, back in her pink-en-crusted room, with her brother Justin out in the hallway attempting—without much luck—to teach Chonger the very American skill of mocking anyone who appeared slightly different, with Addy tightly squeezing Yarnkin and gently slow-dancing to Spandau Ballet's "True," a song that just *had* to have been written *especially* for her, her father downstairs hard at work creating a new advertising campaign for garbage food sold throughout the world at incredibly reasonable prices to college students and the middle-aged who'd long ago given up, and with Addy's mother in the kitchen drunkenly chopping spinach for an imaginary Caesar salad, that it all, finally, began to seem real.

And it would be at that very moment that Addy knew—without a shadow of a doubt, as sure as she ever knew about anything—that before the year was over, a certain sophomore named Addy Stevenson would be attending the prom with a certain senior Roland McDough, he of the north side of the lake.

Roland McDough, he had a lot of dough.

And he would soon have a lot of Addy.

Addy (still stranded on Planet Hormone within the Electric Salamander) closed her eyes and—swaying gently from side to side—began to daydream about an amazing future that had all but seemed impossible mere moments before.

Addy felt as if she were now riding a grinning dolphin beneath a Fruit-Roll-Up-hued rainbow. A pink rabbit sat just off to the side, leisurely playing the lute.

Now he was the one who wasn't wearing pants.

This was *heaven*.

It was French-kissing a setting sun.

CHAPTER THREE

These Modern Contraptions!

It was late afternoon and Addy was in the school's library cramming for the Algebra test to come the following day.

Addy hated Algebra.

She hated any math that didn't involve splitting a dinner check three ways amongst best friends.

Addy placed down her copy of *What Color Are Your Parachute Pants?* She grabbed a seat within the cubicle that held the library's lone computer.

She sighed.

She'd have so much rather been at home alone, in her room, chatting the afternoon away on her banana-shaped phone with Kristina or slow-dancing with Yarn-kin to a moody alternative song featuring mystifying lyrics about succumbing to an early death.

But here she was now, in the library, along with a smattering of other dweebs—

She pressed the computer's huge ON switch. The large screen buzzed to life, shining a deep, futuristic green. It was like the monolith in *2001*, without all the masturbating monkeys.

What did people see in these "computers" anyway? So bulky, so useless ...

28

The screen popped on, flickered for a bit and then stayed on for good. Addy could almost feel the heat emanating from this massive device.

Was it even safe to be this close?

Addy pulled a few practice test papers from out of her backpack. *God how she wished she were just anywhere else but here—*

But wait! What was this?!

Addy watched in shock—but also in utter fascination—as the computer's green screen began to display random, bizarre modern shapes: circles, squares, complicated patterns that started to slowly rotate and intermesh.

What exactly was happening here?!

It was like the opening scene to the movie *Tron*. Without all the masturbating monkeys.

Then this popped up:

"Hey ADDY? You AROUND?"

Huh? Was someone communicating with her—or *trying* to—through the computer?!

She typed:

CMON GRIMER. STOP TEASING.

Not knowing what else to do, she hit the RETURN button.

This was insane!

Could this ever possibly work?

Addy stood and peered over the cubicle at the other students. No one looked her way.

It was the Desolate Land of Shhhhhh.

Sitting back down, Addy noticed that the screen was now displaying the following:

WHOS GRIMER?!

But if this wasn't Grimer ... then who else could it possibly be?

WHO IS THIS? Addy typed with two fingers.

She waited anxiously for the answer to arrive and when it did, she inhaled deeply:

THIS IS ROLAND

But if it was indeed Roland, how was he now talking to her via the computer?!

"HOW ARE OU DOING THIS!" typed Addy, fingers trembling. She was in such a rush that she forgot to type the letter "y" in the word "you."

Addy erased everything she'd just written and retyped the sentence to make more sense.

It was now correct.

Addy tentatively pressed RETURN.

She waited.

Before Addy realized what was happening, stick figures of a boy and a girl appeared on the screen. They were standing a short distance away from each other, and then closer and closer, until finally they were holding hands.

This was magic!

The stick figures began to slow dance.

Addy had never seen anything quite like this.

Addy secretly prayed that these two characters would eventually stop dancing and start smooching. *Wouldn't that have been wild?*

But they quickly did much more.

A stick-figure bed appeared.

The boy stick-figure walked over to it.

The girl stick-figure climbed *into* it.

The boy stick-figure nonchalantly dropped his stick trousers.

Addy had no idea that stick figures could ever be this well endowed.

The girl stick-figure dispassionately took off her stick-figure bra.

Wow. Those ... those were impressive ...

She would never look at crudely line-drawn circles with dots in the middle the same way.

Addy didn't bother to wait to see what happened next.

She left without so much as turning off the computer. She wouldn't have known how anyway.

Addy thought: *Best of luck to the school's one computer nerd tasked with that impossibility!*

CHAPTER FOUR

Lunch Time

The "Hang Gang" sat morosely at their prescribed cafeteria table, the one for the misfits, the Yoids, Zinks, Zats, the Zefs, the Zinky Znus.

There were other tables for rejects—the human equivalents of the unpopped kernels at the bottom of a microwavable popcorn bag—but this was the main table for the losers, the Crankoids, the CrinkCranks, the Jerk Derfs, and even the one true-to-life "Goth," a straight-A student named Danielle who currently went by the darker and more mysterious moniker of "Aurora."

Addy had known and loved most of these friends for years. She felt comfortable with them. Even if no one else did.

In a sense, they were all joined at the "unhip."

Outside, in a specially designated dirt area, were the Smokers, the Metal Heads, the Gearheads, the precocious brown-nosers who still only managed to pull down Cs, and the school's lone super fan of Chris Elliott's *The Fugitive Guy* on *Late Night with David Letterman*. His name was Mike and he was pretty much left alone.

A digital chart hung in the principal's office on the second floor that laid it all out in excruciating detail, updated electronically every three minutes. Students,

the following year, but Cass was, of course, using it first.

Cass's great skill was in predicting, much like a high school Nostradamus, exactly what music, films, and slang would become hugely popular a year into the future—a high school eternity. She was the first to wear a Duran Duran T-shirt, back in seventh grade. She had begged the marching band instructor, Mr. Thompson, to allow them to play "Hungry Like the Wolf," complete with the requisite moaning from the drummers, but he had said no.

As a compromise, the marching band had chosen Prince's ode to all things romantic, "Darling Nikki," to the confusion of both alumni and football fans. Cass was in the rear, tooting happily away on her sousaphone.

Magnus now glanced down at Cass. "How's that *obesa*-phone you play? You know, for the *munching* band?"

"Meaning what?" asked Cass.

"Meaning you have a fat ass," answered Magnus.

"Clever," said Cass. "A real Inspector Gadget. Just *go*. Get the hell out of here."

Magnus apparently understood this—if only barely. He sauntered off, the lapels on his ACA Joe T-shirt erect like two sails headed out to calmer, more understanding seas. When he reached his own table, he leaned down to speak to a curvaceous blonde. Addy saw that this was Jill Standish, currently the school's "number one."

Jill looked over at Addy and shook her head. She wasn't happy. Addy could almost hear the clucking from this far away.

"Any upcoming plans?" asked Cass, off-handedly,

unaware of the negative attention she was receiving from those on the other side of the room. Only Cass could be blissfully unaware of others disliking her. Addy had known Cass since they had first bonded in bible school over their intense hatred for boys with tuna fish bits stuck in their braces.

"*Ugh*," said Addy. "I have to help with my stupid sister's wedding in a few weeks! Same night as prom. The worst!"

"*Same night as prom*?!" asked Kristina, shocked. "How are you going to work *that* out?"

"If Roland asks, I'll just skip my sister's wedding."

They sat in silence—until Kristina finally made a sound, one of utter disgust. "Look who's making his tiny way over!"

"Who?" asked Addy, turning.

"Your younger brother," said Kristina. "Crink Cranking his way straight to our table!"

Justin and his new best buddy, Chonger, approached. On Chonger's tray was a huge mound of crumbled cookies, piled high. It wasn't abundantly clear why.

"Here they come, two Spaz McKenzies," muttered Kristina. "A total nerd herd."

The Chonger was wearing Gasoline Jeans (gray on one side, royal blue on the other), a pair of unlaced red high-top Converse sneakers, an 18th century beaver tri-cornered hat, as well as a pressed-decal T-shirt reading "#1 American!"

It all looked very American.

"*Poozer to the scoozer*!" announced the Chonger, happily. "Jack up to the jack *down*! Time to boogie the all-night fever!"

Without asking permission, Justin and the Chonger sat down at the table, giggling loudly.

"Did anybody invite you?" asked Addy, annoyed.

"Cagney, Lacey!" said Justin to his sister and Kristina. "And the rest of the Hang Gang! How blows it?"

"I'll ask again," said Addy. "Did I *invite* you?"

"Ratty Addy!" retorted Justin. "Didn't need to! Even I, the lowliest of lowly freshmen, know full well that this table does not require an *invitation*."

Chonger laughed very loudly and began spooning cookie crumbs into his mouth.

Kristina, long having already run out of patience, grabbed her tray and backpack.

She stood as if to leave.

Addy made an expression as if to say, *Please don't leave me here alone with these two! C'mon!*

Kristina made an expression back as if to say, *I am more sexually experienced than you! So I have to leave immediately!*

To emphasize this, Kristina pointed to a large, round button she was wearing on her denim overalls that read: "Sex Wanted! Apply Here!!"

And then an arrow down.

It made the point.

"Hey! Chonger," Justin screamed, ignoring Kristina as she hurriedly walked out of the cafeteria. "Show everybody at the school what I just taught you to do!"

The Chonger walked over to an area of the floor between two cafeteria tables and sat down hard. Grabbing his ankles with both hands, he launched into a modern break-dancing "spin." Meanwhile, Justin—standing next to him—counted off a funky, rhythmic black "rap" speech. It sounded slinky and urban.

"*A-one* ... and *a-two* ... and *a-three* ... and *a-kick it!*"

Before long, the entire cafeteria stood watching, in awed silence.

Addy could have like died.

Rippling and thrusting, the Chonger now "wormed" his way across the cafeteria's floor, weight shifting fluidly from his lower to his upper body, over and over and over again.

In no time, the students were laughing *at*—not *with*—Chonger's desire to belong, which was itself very American, but Addy couldn't take it any longer and she quickly grew upset, almost violent, which was also particularly American. She stood to leave ... but stopped suddenly. To quit wasn't very American. *Or was it?* Addy didn't know. Being confused was American, she knew that. She was confused.

And *shocked*.

Because staring at her now, from just a few yards away, was Roland himself. He glanced down at Chonger and then back over to Addy.

Danielle the Goth grinned. This entire scene reminded her of the lyrics to a song by one of her favorite bands, Mission of Burma, minus any references to "dead pools of unending blackness."

Roland gave a relaxed smirk to Addy and coolly shrugged. *Follow me ...*

As if in a pink-hued dream, Addy trailed Roland from out of the cafeteria's doors and into the hallway, past the automatic hair-styling-foam-dispenser attached to the wall. There were fifteen of these dispensers located throughout the school, and one even in the nurse's office for high-style emergencies.

"Hello," said Roland.

"Hi," said Addy.

So far, so good!

"Roland," Addy said. "Were you the one communicating with me yesterday on the computer?"

"Maybe," Roland answered, impishly.

"How did you become so proficient?" asked Addy, genuinely curious.

"My father has one for his home use," Roland replied, no big deal.

"For the *home*?" inquired Addy. She had never heard of such a thing.

"Yeah, you know. For *games*. And, I don't know, for spreadsheets or something," said Roland.

Addy didn't know what to make of all this. Her father, like most grown men, used paper and pen.

"I'm sorry that the computer thing got so out of control," continued Roland. "I guess I pushed the wrong button, I don't know."

"That's okay," said Addy. "I left before anything *too* weird happened."

"I was wondering," Roland continued, barely listening, "I was wondering if I might possibly interest you in attending a party with me this weekend."

He was asking as if practicing before the mirror. Addy found it sweet and endearing.

"Where?" asked Addy.

Where?!

How stupid! But it was the only thing Addy could think to say!

"At my house," answered Roland. "North of the northeast part of the lake."

"I've heard about that area," Addy said, lamely.

"Never been?" asked Roland, knowing full well she hadn't.

"Never," said Addy. "The houses are ... very large."

Very large? What was wrong with her?!

"Yes. They are," Roland said.

Yes, they are?! thought Addy. *How stupid!*

Wait. She hadn't said that. Roland had.

On second thought, it was *adorable*.

Addy had never been more in love in her entire life, and that included her long-term crush on the British alternative pop star Boy George. But sadly, and last she had heard on the afternoon Q101 drive-time show, the George was already seriously involved with a very special, beautiful adult female.

Sigh.

That's not to say Addy had never had any crushes on boys who were more *attainable*.

There was Marc Robinson from Wisconsin summer camp. Addy had held hands with Marc two summers ago next to a campfire. They kissed while wearing orthodontic headgear tightened with the latest in Velcro technology.

Pathetically, that had been Addy's last kiss.

Before that, Addy had kissed only one other boy—or *nearly* kissed. It was Eric McSorley, from sixth grade, who once threw a plastic baggie filled with Elmer's Glue at Addy during recess when she was with friends gossiping and he was taking a break from kickball, but just in the *way* he threw that bag of glue and just in the beautiful fact that he had been paying *any* attention to her ... Addy just *knew*.

Addy still often thought about Eric McSorley. He moved away after his dad was caught in an alleged male prostitution scandal.

She dug his free spirit. Was he *still* throwing bags of glue at his crushes?

"Well, what have we *here*?" asked a voice, seemingly from out of nowhere.

Addy instantly knew who it was even before glancing over immediately.

Grimer. God!

Who else? What terrible timing!

"Hi," said Roland, graciously extending a hand. "My name is Roland. I think we met the other night at the mall. You were riding a unicycle? You smelled like burnt hair and frozen orange juice concentrate?"

"Don't remember," responded Grimer, all slick and cool, absentmindedly scratching at forehead burns, now discharging a yellow, gelatinous pus.

Grimer was dressed in an oversized Hawaiian T-shirt, Bermuda shorts, rainbow suspenders, droopy black socks, as well as a pair of homemade mental hospital slippers, laces long since removed.

The entire outfit was so very '80s *alternative*!

"Roland," said Addy, a bit hesitantly. "This is the Grimer. Grimer, this is Roland."

"I know who he is," said Grimer, sullenly. "Mister Perfection, himself. A real *Sylvester Stallone*!"

Roland ignored him. "My mother was originally from the southwest side of the lake if that makes you feel any better," Roland said humbly, only trying to be friendly.

"It doesn't," replied the Grimer, lamely.

The disparity between these two was so gigantic as to be almost frightening. For the briefest of moments, Addy felt a tad sorry for Grimer, but it only took one whiff of the kid's forehead burns to quickly grow furious once again.

"Well," said Roland, smiling gently and looking at Addy. "I'll see you this Saturday. Will pick you up at 8:00."

"Don't you want to know where I live?" Addy asked, trying to sound provactive. It came off sounding more like Dustin Hoffman in *Tootsie*.

"I already know where you live," answered Roland, turning and walking down the hallway to his next class, Just Enough Spanish to Converse with the Help.

The smell of DRAKKAR "Yes, I Cost $15!" cologne was left in Roland's dreamy wake. To Addy, it smelled of ... *high-end wind*.

"Wait!" she called after him. "I'll meet you at *your* house, okay?!"

Addy was terribly ashamed of her upper-middle-class household and never wanted Roland to come anywhere *close* to it, not that he ever would.

"Don't you want to know where *I* live?" Roland asked, impishly.

"I *already* know!" replied Addy, confidently.

And then less confidently: "Actually, yes. Where do you live?"

"One North Lake View Drive," he answered, winked, and walked away.

"Creep," said Grimer, after Roland disappeared down the hall. "He's following you! He knows where you live! And that stupid name, *Roland*! That's not a name! That's a ..."

Grimer attempted to think of a line that would not only be hilarious but one that would be long remembered. There was a look of supreme concentration on his face.

"...that's a dissolving tablet for diarrhea relief!"

Grimer grimaced.

Even *he* knew he had widely missed the mark with that one.

"I think it's *romantic*," said Addy, a bit defensively. "The most romantic thing anyone's *ever* done!"

Than lighting your hair on fire? thought Grimer, but kept it to himself.

"How could you, Addy?!" he whined. "How could you fall in love with someone like *that*? This guy's always been a huge bore!"

"I'm not sure," said Addy, a bit petulantly. "But he's so beautiful! Those eyelashes. I could watch him in front of his locker checking out his reflection in a Huey Lewis compact disc case *all* day!"

"I just don't get it," burbled Grimer. "*Roland*. That's not a name. That's a ..."

Grimer was going to give it one last shot.

"That's a needle to insert into the penis if you're suffering from impotence."

Grimer was definitely not on his "name game" today. *He'd have to think more on this.*

"Call me later," said Addy. "And leave a message on my new answering machine tape. It's in rap form. *'I ain't here, didn't I just make that clear? ...'* It is *hilarious*!"

"I will," said Grimer, moodily. "Where you headed?"

"To math class with generic formulas written on the blackboard."

"Wait," said Grimer. "I need to tell you something."

Addy stopped, turned.

"Yes?" she asked.

"Meet me at the front of the school tomorrow morning at 7:00. You're playing hooky. And don't tell me you're too busy. I know for a fact that tomorrow's an easy day for you."

"And how would you know that?" asked Addy. "You been spying on me, Grimer?"

Grimer was already making his way down the hallway, the *whish-whoosh, whoosh-whish* of his handcrafted mental hospital slippers echoing soothingly.

Maybe Grimer isn't so bad after all, Addy thought. *He and I will always be great friends. At least until we graduate and I won't see him again until the fifteenth or twentieth reunion when we make a few minutes of uncomfortable small talk by the hummus table and I then come up with a really lame pretext to excuse myself in order to go and see if Roland has aged well.*

But Addy's wondrous reverie did not last long. She emerged from out of her daydream to find Chonger

44

"worm dancing" his way out of the cafeteria, his inner-city slithering all frenetic and spastic.

He circled around Addy, one, twice, three times.

That did it.

Addy marched straight off to algebra class, the one taught by the familiar looking teacher whose name she could never remember but with the recognizable face that could very well have been in any number of teen films.

Placing her miniature cassette player "Walkman" feather-light headphones over her ears, she began listening to one of her all-time favorite *alterna* songs.

It was called "Popped Collar Nights" and it was almost as if it was written *especially* for her:

I met you at the party where I didn't belong.
We danced all night to what became our favorite song.
But when the lights came back on and it was time to go,
How could I tell the truth? How could I let you know?

Popped collar nights!
The princess and the pauper from the other side!
Popped collar nights!
Two caste aways in love who must forever hide!

A whole new world out there I had never known.
The dinners, boats and country clubs your family owned!

We lived the lie and reached up to the highest of heights.
Undercover love on endless summer nights!

Popped collar nights!
It's how they live on the other side!
Popped collar nights!
To roll the dice, to walk with pride!

And now you tell me we can never be.
But that's the others talking, that's not you or me!
Nobody else out there for me but you!
Won't ever let you go 'cause my love is true!

Popped collar nights!
I'll be by your side all night and day!
Popped collar nights!
Be watchin' if you even think of goin' away!

Popped collar nights!
The princess and the pauper from the other side!
Popped collar nights!
Two caste aways in love who must forever hide!

CHAPTER FIVE

Adventure Time

The next morning Grimer had been true to his word and had met Addy outside the entrance to their school at precisely 7:00, which was only a few minutes after Addy's father had dropped her off 500 yards farther than anyone of any importance could ever see her exiting that stupid Tweedledumb Volvo.

Her father blew her a kiss.

Whatever.

When Grimer had pulled up, he was driving a priceless Ferrari.

Only one of its kind ever made.

Worth at least $15 million.

Convertible.

So sleek.

Gorgeous.

An automobile that no policeman would ever think of stopping, especially driven erratically by a teenager with severe forehead burns and wild, unfocused eyes...

...or so the Grimer had implied when Addy had climbed in.

"Isn't it *fabulous*, Addy?"

"It's ... very nice," responded Addy, who didn't know much about cars but did know a Chevy Nova when she sat in one.

Sometimes it was just best to play along with Grimer's moony delusions that did not always strictly adhere to what the rest of the world might call "facts."

"Do you even have a license?" Addy had asked, as they pulled away.

"Yes," Grimer said.

Another delusion. Maybe it *wasn't* always best to play along.

"Did you steal this?"

"Yup," said Grimer. "For the day. From the school parking lot. It's Mr. Hollingsworth's, the gym teacher's."

"Do you want me to drive?" Addy had asked, a bit worried.

That last car bump hadn't felt good.

"You don't have a license either," extorted Grimer, weaving in and out of traffic, running over what just had to be—*Addy prayed*—another small suburban road critter.

"True," she said, smiling.

Addy knew very little about Grimer. *He was exceedingly mysterious. Where did he live? Was his house larger than 5,000 square feet? Why did he keep running over small animals? Was there a reason he was wearing a purple shirt beneath a pink leather jacket and a green beret?*

Today would be a wonderful opportunity to learn more about this strange, fetid creature …

"You want to tell me where we're headed?" Addy asked.

"Gosh, I have *so* many things planned," announced

nessmen glancing out their high rise office windows, including a certain advertising copywriter who did a doubletake when he saw a girl who looked exactly like his daughter, which was all but impossible, as she was still in school, *she never skipped!*

"What's he singing to?" asked another man who was wearing a yarmulke.

The yarmulke, as was the latest craze, was acid washed and 100% "pre shrunk."

"A horrible song in his head," said a businessman, struggling to be heard over the screams. Grimer was dancing and singing on top of a car, its hood now beginning to dish in the middle.

Miming playing the knee cymbals, both knees clashing, Grimer screamed out: "*Clang, clang, clang-a-dang, clang-a-dang a-rang!*"

"Guy's off his rocker," said a construction worker, sadly. "Nuttier than the goddamn stones in Reagan's head!"

It was slowly dawning on Addy that something might not be quite "right" with her good friend, Grimer, who was now laughing hysterically, can-canning and bowing.

"You insufferable, smarmy jackass!" yelled a middle-aged woman to Grimer. "You're not cute! You're a horror show!"

Addy figured now might be as good a time as any to go and retrieve the Chevy Nova. If she waited any longer, she feared, Grimer might very well be shot to death.

Minutes later, Addy had returned with the worthless Chevy Nova, parking it just a few feet from where

Grimer was pirouetting and lip-synching, windmilling his arms and flapping them like a freshly-hatched duckling.

Addy beeped the car's horn.

Grimer glanced over.

Grimer saw a hovering, flying monster with a large tail and a huge spiked horn, blowing a saucy kiss and sticking out its narrow, forked green tongue ...

Grimer smiled.

But then looked closer.

Addy?

Wanting to leave?!

Huh?!

Grimer angrily jumped down off the car's collapsed roof and stomped his irritable way over to the Chevy Nova.

"What are you *doing*, Addy?!" Grimer screamed. "These people are *adoring* my antics!"

"They are," said Addy, very slowly. "But ... it's quite late and I must be home. What a wonderful day, though! Get in please."

"Truly, Addy?" said Grimer, climbing into the passenger seat. "You honestly thought today was wonderful? Did I *wow* you?"

Did he wow me? thought Addy.

"The best day I've spent in *forever*," replied Addy, opening her window, breathing deeply. The smell in the car was incomparable.

Screeches and howlings could be heard, evidently from a woman being forced to give birth in the backseat of her 1975 Mellow Yellow AMC Gremlin because of

"I'll just walk. There's so much to think about before tomorrow's party at Roland's, anyway."

"The school it is," said Grimer, falling back into silence.

A song could be heard coming from the car's cassette player. It featured no lyrics.

Addy thought, *If this song were to ever be featured on a movie soundtrack, it would definitely be on side two, towards the end.*

Way *towards the end.*

If at all.

At one point, Grimer suggested they attempt to drive in reverse in order to turn back the miles on the odometer, but then thought better of it: the last time he had driven in reverse without a license he had come very close to killing someone—luckily it had just been a shithead in a leased DeLorean.

There was also very little chance that Mr. Hollingsworth, the gym teacher, would ever question why there were an extra 24 miles on his 1978 Chevy Nova. He had much more important things to worry about: like covering up his affair with the seventeen-year-old daughter of Mr. Dufournaud, the civics teacher.

When Addy and Grimer finally arrived back at school, in a haze of exhaust, the parking lot was empty. Addy had no problem finding a space.

Night had fully descended.

"See you Monday," said Addy casually, leaving the keys in the ignition, exiting the car along with Grimer. There was no point in unbuckling their seatbelts. They hadn't to begin with. They hadn't wanted to look like idiots. "I'll be sure to have plenty of war stories about the party!"

"Addy," said Grimer, sadly. "Oh, Addy." He was now backlit by a dull beam of an overhead yellow light that created a halo around his very carefully constructed hair wave. He looked angelic.

"Yes?" asked Addy.

"Were you serious about having a good time today?"

"I was," said Addy. "I had a *wonderful* time, Grimer."

Grimer gave a limp smile, his first since suffering a concussion at the hands of the Polish-American day-trader with anger issues.

"Have fun at the party."

"I shall," said Addy. "I *hope* to anyway."

Grimer crouched with his left arm draped across a knee. He looked like an extra in a bad Shakespeare production. The type prone to making a dramatic show of every little movement and yet a character who says and does absolutely nothing of any importance.

"M'lady, I think thee shall do doth *fine*."

Addy laughed. "You're *certifiable*, Grimer."

"Only crazy for *thee*," Grimer replied.

Addy sighed. "Sorry, my friend. Just not in the cards."

"Fun have," said Grimer, standing up from his kneeling position.

He had done it again. Modernized and freshened a clichéd greeting by reversing the order!

"Thanks. I'll let you know how it goes."

"Then until," said Grimer.

"Until then," said Addy, smiling.

58

Wordlessly, they looked at each other mutely.

Perhaps a bit *too* long.

Addy closed her eyes, breaking the spell.

She made her way down an empty street towards home, eyes still closed.

The entire day had truly been horrendous, one of the worst ever, but there was also something ... *romantic* about it all. She'd be lying if she didn't admit that she really *did* love and crave all the attention, even if Grimer *had* forced a woman to give premature birth in the back of a 1975 Mellow Yellow AMC Gremlin.

When Addy eventually opened her eyes and turned around to see if Grimer was still posed in his useless Shakespearean position, the weirdo was nowhere to be seen.

He'd virtually disappeared.

A rare and strange creature, this one. There was so much to love. And yet ...

Addy decided to think about it all later. Her eyes still hurt from observing that middle-aged guy "sky-toinkling" himself at the top of the Sears tower.

But, more than anything, she had a party outfit to plan!

Addy again closed her eyes ... and ricocheted home off the dream-jam.

CHAPTER SIX

Party Time!

Saturday evening. 9:59 P.M.

Addy stood before the long, winding, white-concrete driveway that led straight to the nearly all-glass mansion at the top of the hill.

Did she really want to do this? It was so much easier to do ... *nothing*. To merely stay at home and daydream about such events. So much simpler to just float down the stream, within its trouble-free margins, without all the ripples and currents and all the annoying bits of debris that could potentially harm. Who was she to even *come* to this party? Addy was so north of the lake that she was nearly suffering the bends.

Her father had dropped her off a half mile away in his Tweedledumb Volvo.

"Have a new fast-food slogan," he had said to Addy. "Want to hear it? Great: This freak in a white suit and bolo tie says: 'I definitely ain't a Colonel, never was, but my chicken, it sure is factory farm delicious!'"

Addy smiled.

"Sure, daddy."

Whatever.

She then wished him the best of luck as he began the dangerous 5.2 mile drive back to their average upper-middle-class shit hole on the wrong side of the lake.

"Enjoy yourself!" enfeebled her father, blowing Addy a kiss.

As for Addy's outfit ... she truly considered it her *magnum opus*, a word she once heard while watching *Reading Rainbow* and later wrote down in her "NEW WORD & PHRASE JOURNAL."

It was the only entry.

The journal, itself, was covered in blue sparkle and silver tinsel, and it was *spectacular*. Addy would have to add a new word before she eventually graduated. Or convert it into some other type of journal, perhaps one devoted to her *least* favorite guest stars to ever appear on *The Love Boat*, beginning with Ernő Rubik, the elderly Hungarian inventor of the Rubik's Cube, who sat seductively on the Lido Deck, wearing only a skimpy red, blue, white, orange, green, and yellow Speedo.

Addy took mental stock of herself.

Every item of tonight's outfit had originated from another source: a pink and white speckled frock she had purchased that looked like an outfit Laura Ingalls would have worn to a rustic prairie *bat mitzvah;* a pair of dangling art deco earrings fashioned out of two weathered clothespins stolen from an elderly neighbor's line; a silk elbow-length glove on her left arm, stolen from that same elderly neighbor's "Memories To Last a Lifetime!" trunk; and a small brocade clutch purse that was, in reality, just a plastic take-out baggy from The Ground Round and smelled vaguely of "lake shrimp."

Addy silently thanked the homeless people in downtown Chicago. It was from their varied and colorful experiences and one-of-a-kind outfits that she drew her inspiration for her implausible, forward-thinking designs.

But what Addy was most proud of was the gorgeous pearl necklace her father had ceremoniously draped around her neck just before she got into the car for the ride to the party.

"The pearls are so *beautiful*," Addy had declared. "I've never seen them before. Oh, *daddy*!"

"They're your mother's," her father had replied. "She keeps it in her dirty underwear drawer. I snuck it out this morning when she was too drunk to care. She's still too drunk to care."

It was one of the most beautiful things her father had ever told her and she would not soon forget it.

Addy now looked up at the party taking place on top of the hill. It was already in full jazzy-swing ... just like she always imagined it would be.

She wondered what her "Hang Gang" was doing right this very instant. Kristina, no doubt, was on a date with a fifty-something at an upscale chain-restaurant with hilariously useless and rusting knick-knacks and gee-gaws hanging from the walls. Lucy was most likely at home, alone in her bedroom, taking intimate Polaroids of her pet mantis Miss Verde, as well as of her numerous and fancy ant farms. Cass was also undoubtedly alone—*who else would she be with?*—watching bootleg VHS tapes of British comedy programs that wouldn't appear on American TV until the following year, if at all.

This was Addy's group. She missed them desperately.

But she also felt as if she had no other choice but to be here now.

She was like an astronaut who had been sent out on a dangerous mission to colonize the sun. But perhaps even braver. There would be no parades or crowds upon her return.

The house's tremendously large front lawn, sloping down and out to the wide, Dutch-Elm-Diseased-Dutch-Elm-lined street, was packed with hundreds, possibly thousands, of attractive high school students, cavorting, capering, prancing, and, in one unfortunate case, gamboling.

Addy had heard of such parties but had never personally observed one up close. Up until this very moment, she had always thought them to be a myth.

Or a bad joke.

Like that time a group of Populars had invited her to a party at a house far, far away. When she arrived at the front door with a present she had bought with her own babysitting money—a paperback copy from *The Sweet Dreams* series—no one would open.

Because they couldn't hear her.

It was an old-age home.

She had been given the wrong address.

When they finally did let her in, the residents didn't allow her to leave for days.

But this was different.

Oh, how this was different!

What Addy was now seeing was *spectacular*.

The scene was like something out of a movie written by a man who had never once attended a high school

63

party.

Addy felt as if she were floating. To her left, a couple in matching white-and-black-checkerboard-patterned outfits kissed. To her right, a boy she recognized from last year's English class was carrying piggyback a girl she recognized from this year's remedial sex ed. A girl to her left was passed out, arms splayed, clutching a Tiffany lamp. A boy to her right respectfully raised a penis-shaped candle to the night sky—a most special offering to the teen gods.

Girls in fur coats. *Pinks in minks.*

Boys in button-downs. *Blues in crews.*

Everyone was here!

Addy could see inside the packed, nearly vibrating glass house.

So many students having the time of their young lives! Almost *too many*! Addy wondered how she would ever manage to locate Roland …

She needn't have worried.

Swaggering from out of the house was Roland himself clutching two Champagne flutes, one in each hand, both filled to the brim. His smile was huge. Addy took a step back, almost as if being knocked backwards by a delicious, ferocious wind.

His cologne was nearly as powerful as Van Damme's muscles!

And as invigorating!

"Hello," Roland said when he at least reached her.

"Hello," Addy said in return.

So far, so good.

"How did you even know I was here? It's so crowded

with ... *people*."

"I've been waiting. You know, just for you."

Addy caught another smell. Whether it was Roland's shampoo, or his fancy deodorant, or even his tobacco-scented aftershave, Malignancy, it was *bewitching*. When it mixed with the smell of her Clearasil, it became a new intoxicating odor, one potentially never smelled before on Earth.

"I brought you some Champagne," Roland announced, handing over to Addy a glass overflowing with expensive bubbly. Addy didn't see any remnants of a price tag on the glass, nor were there any Chicago sports team logos on it. This was the *real* deal.

Addy took the tiniest of tiny sips.

"Like it?" Roland asked, eagerly. "$500 a bottle. From the Champagne region in France!"

"I thought *all* Champagne was from the Champagne region in France," Addy replied.

Addy had remembered this amazing bit of trivia from a *Trivial Pursuit* card she once found on a table at a pizzeria. The card was filthy. In retrospect, she never should have touched it. There was a pretty good chance it had given her strep.

Roland said nothing. And then with that most *delightful* amount of imperiousness, he exclaimed: "Follow!"

With Roland's hand possessively on her back, Addy—still gripping the finely-stemmed toasting flute—eagerly allowed this gorgeous Richie to lead her up to the glass house, beckoning so alluringly.

The place was glass taste architecturalized!

Addy stepped through the large front entrance,

directly into an alternate universe, one of vibrancy and extraordinary spectacle. To Addy, it was exactly like that famous scene in *The Wizard of Oz,* a movie Addy always despised because it featured physically stunted actors who were neither handsome nor beautiful, and because the supposedly ten-year-old Dorothy had much larger breasts than Addy now had as a fifteen-year-old.

What Addy saw within this great house was like nothing she had ever witnessed! One miraculous sight after another appeared before her eyes!

She saw:

Pyramids, 15 feet high, created with only empty beer cans!

Smoke from tobacco-cigarettes wafting to the glass rafters above!

Large athletic types placing compact discs into compact disc players!

Half-naked women, their breasts jingling and jangling, perched on the shoulders of college football players!

Pizza pies, half-eaten, lazily strewn across expensive white-leather couches!

Two twenty-something men screaming: "BOOGA-DA-BOOGADA-BOOGOODA, AHH-AHH-AHH!"

A fat biker with a beard pouring vodka into a crystal punch bowl!

A Preppie with his "stink finger" extended, all fancy-like!

A miniature show horse with a crimped and permed tail held back with a pink scrunchie!

Addy guessed this must be the infamous "Whinny."

Even the miniature horse, appeared indifferent!

Addy blinked. "Is this *happening*? I mean, really *happening*?"

She tried to take all of it in at once: the muscle-bound men playing poker who looked as if they had been directly beamed in from the latest issue of *Gentlemen's Quarterly.*

And over there ... a professional escort wearing a Kentucky Derby hat, licking caviar straight from out of her own palms.

"*Unquestionably,*" replied Roland, slowly. "This is *unquestionably happening!*"

Addy continued to gape.

A woman's brassiere was hanging from out of an elaborate gilt art frame. To Add.. to be at least a double A.

Ice-blue satin strapless..

And over there, h..

a jock strap, a r..

crocodile s..

prim..

teu..

She n..

Maybe tha..

"Roland," said o..

wearing trendy clothing ..

Addy's father earned in an enu..

this?" he asked. He was pulling his r..

down to the tip of his nose, Tom Cruise-s..

He had obviously performed this move bei..

It went off without a hitch.

Another swank male, a real "Joe Community College" type—donning a velour Fila tracksuit and gently nibbling a cocktail onion at the end of a mono-grammed silver toothpick—quipped: "More like, *what* is this?"

"*Gauche,*" creampuffed another. "Total art fag. What is *happening*, homes?"

"Feather plucker," murbled yet another Richie.

"And what exactly is she *wearing*?" asked a Popu-lar Girl, smiling tightly. "I mean, *really*! It looks like something that Max Headroom would have t-t-t-t-thrown up!"

The boy who had previously been introduced as Pribbenow laughed. "Babe," he said. "Babe, is this a *gaggers*? A *yukkers*?" He foppishly tossed back a single strand of hair from his forehead. "You're wasting your $500 Champagne on a ... non-lake *girl*?!"

"This is *Addy*," said Roland patiently. "And she is my date tonight to the party."

"This *has to be* a put-upon!" quiched Camilla, a short brunette wearing a sequined lace taffeta gown.

A handsome boy—Addy knew him to be the scho[ol] star debater—was loudly speechifying with hi[s ...] about the pros and cons of underage drinking. T[he] side was clearly coming out ahead, if a bit dis[...]

Hooza! This was all very much *happeni[ng]*

"Very much *happening*," emphasized [...]

"This place," said Addy excitedly. "[...]

"I know. Right this way. I want to [...] some of my good friends."

Addy adjusted her silk elbow[...] left arm. She really did wish to [...] impression you made with a R[...] your *last!*

Roland guided Addy o[...] chatting behind a treme[...]

This group looked

"Addy. I'd like you to [...] clockwise around the small circ[...]

"This is Blaize, Dashiell, Magnu[s] and Barron. And this is Huxley, Pribbenow, Bullion, and Akdov Telmig, a Russian. And [...] Roland gestured before the entire group, "*this* is my date for the evening, Addy Stevenson."

She had met Magnus before, he of the "Titty Committee."

"Hi," announced Addy.

There was silence.

Uh oh.

Was "hi" not correct? Would "hello" have been more Ramba appropriate? There were too many rules of etiquette! And no one had ever taken the time to

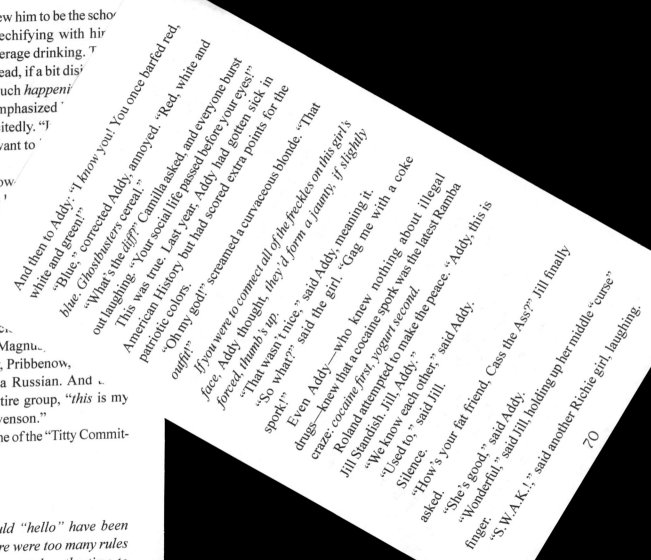

And then to Addy: "*I know you!* You once barfed red, white and green!"

"Blue," corrected Addy, annoyed. "Red, white and blue. *Ghostbusters* cereal."

"What's the *diff?*" Camilla asked, and everyone burst out laughing. "Your social life passed before your eyes!"

This was true. Last year, Addy had gotten sick in American History but had scored extra points for the patriotic colors.

"Oh my god!" screamed a curvaceous blonde. "That outfit!"

If you were to connect all of the freckles on this girl's face, Addy thought, *they'd form a jaunty, if slightly forced, thumb's up.*

"That wasn't nice," said Addy, meaning it. "Gag me with a coke spork!"

"So what?" said the girl.

Even Addy—who knew nothing about illegal drugs—knew that a cocaine spork was the latest Ramba craze: *cocaine first, yogurt second.*

Roland attempted to make the peace. "Addy, this is Jill Standish. Jill, Addy."

"We know each other," said Addy.

"Used to," said Jill.

Silence.

"How's your fat friend, Cass the Ass?" Jill finally asked.

"She's good," said Addy.

"Wonderful," said Jill, holding up her middle "curse" finger.

"S.W.A.K.!" said another Richie girl, laughing.

Sealed. With. A. Kiss.

This crowd, thought Addy ... *this crowd is playing for* keeps.

"And how's your stupid friend who works in that stupid store?" asked another girl.

Addy recognized her as being Cathy Douglas, the customer who had asked Kristina the other day if the Electric Salamander sold three-pack neon scrunchies.

Addy turned to Roland. "I'm very embarrassed and would like to leave now."

"It's okay. My friends are just kind of jerks when they meet someone from the wrong side of the lake, that's all."

The Wiśniewski Twins, the only twins in the school, and famous throughout the area for having their own language, with more than one hundred different words for "kielbasa," grinned.

"I *really* want to go," Addy said again, louder. "*Please!*"

What would the great Dave Gahan of Depeche Mode do in this situation?

Addy had no idea. She placed her Champagne flute, still filled to the top, down on a fancy end table. Roland did the same. Both glasses were promptly picked up by a senior with an array of ski-lift tickets attached to his bare belly with Scotch Tape, and consumed. He blurted, "Time to get *polluted*!"

"What's the rush-a-doodlies?" declared the boy named Declan, sporting a Bill Blass jacket, minimum cost $95. "Let me *microwave* you a hamburger!"

Was that even possible? Addy's family cooked their

burgers the old fashioned way: by paying the cleaning woman, Hermata, a few extra dollars to stay until past eight before she was driven to the bus station for her nightly three-hour ride back to north Indiana.

"Yeah," said a Richie, it wasn't clear who. "What's the *hurry, Skurry?*"

Addy felt as if the entire party had just come to a screeching halt.

The Richie said it again, this time even louder and without the contraction: "WHAT IS THE HURRY, SKURRY?!"

The dreaded Richie rhyme—only used in those most awkward of situations involving Richies and Non-Richies!

And Addy had just experienced it first hand!

She'd have to tell all her friends that this was very much not *an urban legend!*

Even the miniature show horse, Whinny, glanced over. He appeared bored by it all. This *definitely* wasn't his first high school party ....

Nothing more was said.

Everything hung in the balance.

Until Roland made the first move.

"Nice," said Roland to his friends, as he gently lead Addy away from the group and over to the staircase. "Real nice. *Thanks.*"

He was being sarcastic.

"Don't mention it," said Pribbenow. "Any time, babe."

Laughter.

What boy would actually call another boy "babe"?

72

And if this was done in public, what exactly were Richies capable of saying in *private*?

"Can we please just *go*. *Please*, Roland. I don't belong here! I never should have come this far north!"

"I want to be with you. Let's just go upstairs, okay? Where it's quieter and I can kiss you without being seen or mocked by your social betters."

Addy shot him a look.

"Whoa," responded Roland. "*Innocent*! Look! I have my hands in my pockets! I'm as harmless as a Smurf at a forest orgy! These hands will stay just where they are! I promise!"

Addy grinned. She was starting to feel better—*just a little*, even though Roland's hands did seem to be making slight jerky movements.

"C'mon up the stairs we go now," announced Roland. "I'm just an innocuous church mouse! Roll with ol' Roland here!"

Addy—perhaps against her better judgment—followed a few steps behind Roland towards the stairs, passing Pribbenow.

The guy reminded Addy of the big bully dog in just about any Disney film.

Addy walked up the winding staircase which seemed to go on forever. There was no doubt about it: Roland's father *had* to work a *very* important job to afford a mansion this big.

IBM exec?

Stand-up videogame repairman?

The owner of his own local chain of VHS rental stores?

Whoever the guy was, he had to be making six figures a year!

When Addy and Roland at last reached the second floor, they took a right, and walked down a wide hallway. They passed a bedroom, with its door open all the way.

Addy took a peek inside. This room—it looked to be some sort of guest room, even though it was practically bigger than Addy's entire house—was filled with hundreds of soft-sculptured dolls, each totally different from the rest, all posed in disturbing positions.

"Oh, don't pay any attention to *that*," said Roland, still walking down the hallway. "That's just my dad's pornographic Cabbage Patch collection. A real *weirdo!*"

Addy noticed one particular female doll, in what appeared to be a leather outfit, whipping a male doll who was wearing a suit and tie, cowering while on his lunch break, loving it all.

"And what are those figurines in that glass case?" Addy asked, pointing to three shelves of ceramic men and women.

"X-rated Hummels from the Franklin Mint. Aren't they somethin' *somethin'*?"

Addy looked closer. The Hummels were copulating.

Leather and lace.

Richie Revolting.

Bizarro peppery yum ...

"And here's *my* bedroom!" said Roland at last, opening a door at the end of the hall.

Did any other room in the universe, beside this one, have an unusually large hot tub filled with what looked to be bubbling Diet Tab, and a curving slide dropping

74

directly into its center, perfect for some late-night nude tubbin'?

Roland pulled his hands from out of his pockets—both balmy—and immediately hugged Addy.

"Roland. I ... don't want to kiss tonight."

"Why not?" Roland asked, lips mere centimeters away from Addy's. Addy noticed that each of Roland's nostril hairs was perfectly in place, not one even *slightly* askew, each flawlessly colored, all groomed with what just had to be the world's most expensive nose-hair gel.

She had once read about this most modern and European look in a *Sassy* letter-to-the-editor.

"I just think it might be too soon."

"Well, what on Earth are you waiting for? I mean, *what exactly*? I *like* you. And you like me, right?"

"I don't know, maybe ... wouldn't it be better if the first kiss happened prom night?"

But Addy didn't get the sentence out. She could no longer speak.

Roland's sumptuous lips were pressed tightly against hers! And they were *moving*. And separating. His breath smelled of expensive lake oysters: penetrating, brackish, with just a pinch of danger and food poisoning. The only chinchilla at a failing downtown pet store.

Roland's handsome tongue was slowly sliding out of his own and about to enter *her* mouth—

"Stop!" beseeched Addy, pulling away, breaking down in tears. "I don't get it! *I don't get any of it!* Why me? *Why*?!"

Roland, with his hands back in his pockets and pumping ever faster, answered: "I don't know, Addy!

Just *cause*!"

He appeared *forlorn*, even though he himself would never have used that specific word.

Roland had long ago planned on hiring a *polymath* to take the ACT standardized test for him.

That was also a word or phrase he'd never use. He preferred: "Smart Kid Willing to Take Someone Else's Test for Cash."

"It's just ... oh, I don't know! I *like* you. Isn't that *enough*?" Roland declared, appearing genuinely hurt.

Addy began to answer ... but stopped when she heard a scream. It was piercing; it was *against nature*.

Roland heard it too. He now faced a most difficult choice: attempt to kiss Addy again, try to stick his gorgeous, taut tongue into her mouth ... or head downstairs to see if his mother's priceless Steuben glass egg was safe. His mother had purchased it at half-price a few weeks back from a killer Chicago pimp named Guido. She hadn't asked any questions. She never did.

Roland decided to kiss Addy again.

But Addy was having none of it. "Stop trying to kiss me and find out where that scream is coming from!" she screamed at Roland.

Roland appeared upset.

Typical Yoid! Bourgeois concerns about strangers dying painful deaths!

But what else could he do?

It was his *house, after all. Would money really mean nothing to him if he didn't care about a Yoid death?*

Roland took off, running down the stairs, taking two steps at a time.

Addy was just behind on the glass steps, moving with a lot less grace and rubber-outsoled elegance. Her wedged espadrilles just weren't designed for high-priced adventure.

A dog came bounding up to Addy at the foot of the stairs, tail wagging. Addy noticed that one of the dog's front toe nails appeared to be longer than all the others.

"Cocaine nail," someone murmured.

Addy nodded. She should have known. The dog was wearing a porkpie hat pushed back on its head to highlight a carefully constructed "crazy gelled" wave.

Didn't Grimer have a similar look?

The living room had been cleared for a giant game of spin-the-bottle. The guests had formed a huge circle, alternating boy, girl, boy, girl, ending with the miniature horse, still looking all cool and nonplussed.

This definitely wasn't this horse's first game of spin-the-bottle ...

Addy tentatively moved closer to the circle, hoping against all hope to not get sucked into the gravitational, hormonal free-for-all. It was truly disgusting, this public display of affection. It reminded Addy of her least favorite animal, the peacock. Too hungry by half. Colorful feathers all erect, so entitled, so *in your face.* Calm the hell down, you know? Show some restraint! *Couldn't all animals in heat just show their gaudy, stiff feathers in private and be done with it?*

Addy moved even closer ... and gulped.

The participants were *not* using a bottle.

The participants were spinning a *human being,* around and around, and kissing whoever happened to

77

be in the direction of this human's head.

The human was Chonger.

Chonger was screaming very loudly. It was a scream of pure joy:

"Very clever game! Chonger just want to kiss American girlfriend! No monkey business! Chonger love excitement! Chonger make it *all* happen!"

Addy felt woozy.

Chonger was having a wonderful time and she wasn't?!

She was the American *for crying out loud!*

"Ain't this a panic?" someone next to Addy asked.

A panic?

The Iranian hostage situation.

Reagan's assassination attempt.

People starving to death somewhere or other.

Those were all panics.

But *this?*

This was a nightmare.

Addy felt faint.

Not *cute* faint. *Humiliating* faint. Like that time she had passed out in gym class after learning that Luke and Laura from *General Hospital* didn't exist in "real" life.

"*Wait*, Addy," said Roland, just behind her. "Don't pay any attention to them. My friends are all kind of jerks when they use a foreigner as a sex-game aid!"

"I had you pegged differently."

"You're leaving?" asked Roland, standing next to an ancient African mask in a Plexi display case. He was confused. "But why would you be leaving?"

Addy was already out the front door, past a Well-

78

Heeled Flushy clutching his freshly microwaved hamburger. It smelled so delicious that Addy promised herself that if she ever did graduate from fashion school, majoring in useless knickknacks and earning just enough money selling hand-crafted novelties to lower-middle-class retirees at sad outdoor flea markets in abandoned parking lots, the first thing she would do, besides purchasing anti-depressants, would be to cook herself a microwavable two-pound burger and savor it for hours on her fancy balcony overlooking a lake—*any* lake, even a small and depressing one located smack dab in the middle of disheartening, landlocked Illinois. Addy would show them! *All of them!* One of these days, they'd *all* be sorry! She would become *super successful*. And *famous*! She'd appear on the covers of *Dynamite* and even *Life*! She'd be talked about by the hosts of *Real People* and *Ripley's Believe It or Not*! The most important and well-regarded news outlets on Earth!

Before heading out of the house and down onto the great front lawn, Addy glanced back.

Roland was chatting and laughing with his friends by the house's entrance.

Shouldn't Roland have been more upset that she was leaving? Had she done something wrong? Not worn the appropriate outfit? Should she have even more aggressively faked her laughter?

What did Roland want from her exactly? And how could she provide it?

It was all so confusing!

Addy sprinted down the hill and out onto the Dutch-Elm-Diseased-Dutch-Elm-lined street.

79

She was headed home. Where she belonged. The dangerous mission had failed.

Behind her, Addy heard a gag and then a retch.

Chonger must be suffering the spins.

Addy noticed moss growing on the eastern side of the lawn jockey. Even *he* was wearing Gucci.

Using this as directional guidance—and fleeing southwest—Addy picked up speed and continued on with her most daring escape.

CHAPTER SEVEN

A Very Important Talk

Addy finally stumbled back into her unexceptional 5,000 square-foot Winnetka Georgian household with the huge front-door brass knockers at around 1:00 A.M.

Her gorgeous Ma Ingalls barn-raising outfit was in tatters. She was holding one shoe, which wasn't even hers. It had been lying by the side of the road. It'd come in handy if she ever came across a *second* pink Capezio Jazz shoe lying by the side of the road, next to another fresh car crash.

Addy immediately hit the upholstered living room couch, too tired to even make her way up the carpeted, non-glass stairs.

Within seconds, her father—dressed only in a blue putter-tattered bathrobe—was hovering over her in a most "fatherly" fashion. Addy could have cried even harder.

Why her?!

"Wasn't I supposed to pick you up?" he asked, confused.

Typical father!

"I never called, daddy!"

"Right," her father said, eyes glazing into the middle distance. "What's the matter, Addy? You're holding one shoe that doesn't belong to you. Is everything okay?"

"Everything's fine," cried Addy. "Everything's just hunky dory with ol' Addy Stevenson!"

"Aw, c'mon now," said her father. "I can read you better than that."

This conversation was really the last thing Addy now needed. *To answer questions from her own father! Way too many questions. The guy was a real Geraldo Rivera!*

She just wanted to feel sorry for herself. *Couldn't a girl do that anymore without being bothered?! Any particular reason her father wasn't picking up on her verbal cues!*

"It's a boy, daddy. *Okay*?!"

"Okay, okay," said her father calmly. "I used to be a boy once!"

"You were never a Richie," said Addy. "How would you *ever* understand?"

"Oh, I see," said her father. "Problems with a *Richie* boy."

"Oh, *daddy*! This one, he's the most beautiful and perfect senior at school!"

Addy's father took a seat at the end of the couch by Addy's feet.

"Talk to your ol' man. What's the matter? You're crying. And you're holding one shoe that doesn't belong to you. Is everything okay?"

"You've said that already, daddy!"

"I loathe life, honey. I'm so very tired. Tired *to* death, anxious *for* death."

Addy wasn't sure she could continue. She was *that* upset. But somehow she knew that if she were to push

82

hard—beyond the extended limits, beyond the scope of what she ever thought possible—she could somehow get through all this madness, this insanity.

In her mind, Addy often liked to imagine she was Anne Frank, bravely carrying on in spite of all the stupid stuff constantly swirling around her.

"Addy, I'd like to apologize," continued her father. "I forgot the anniversary of your first period. That's not right. But I've a lot on my mind."

"Like the princess getting married?" asked Addy.

"Yes," said her father, looking pained. "Like that. You two are so different. To be honest, she is more attractive. And you're ... more adept at producing useless but creative curios. As for your brother, well, what can I say? But that's no excuse."

"That's okay, daddy. I understand," Addy replied quietly.

Was it okay? Even she didn't know anymore. "Maybe for the *second* anniversary of my first period," she finished, trying to sound helpful.

"And as for our new transfer student from Czecho-slovakia—"

"China, daddy."

"Maybe," said her father. "Now, as for this boy, why don't you just ask him to prom yourself?"

"Oh, daddy! You *really* don't understand!" she cried out, bursting into tears. "Princess Mary's wedding is on prom night! I couldn't go even if I *wanted* to!"

"Honey," said her father, gently patting his daughter's splattered frock. "*It's my turn, okay?* If this boy could see all of the wonderful things that I can see about

83

you—like your bloody shoes from whatever the hell happened on that long walk home, or your mood swings that can viciously switch within even the same sentence, or the disturbing way in which you self-hug and dance yourself around your bedroom feeling incredibly sorry for yourself, or all of those countless, endless hours you spend on that telephone in the shape of a banana talking to god knows who as treacly New Wave music blasts in the background—well, if he can't see that, *then I feel sorry for this boy!*"

Addy giggled. Her father was *right*. She *did* have a lot to offer! And if this Richie couldn't see how wonderful she was with his own stupid, gorgeous eyes, she'd just have to move on to another Richie with stupid, gorgeous eyes!

"But there's a *second* boy who likes me," said Addy. "His name is the Grimer. And he's ... so ... *mysterious*."

"Tell me about him," said her father in a genuine manner, half listening.

"Well ... he loves to do fun things. Like wearing interesting clothing and to dance on top of cars and lip-synch to all the old-fashioned songs in his head that really amuse the owners of all the cars he's damaging ..."

Her father's brow furrowed. "This ... *boy*, Addy? He didn't happen to be in downtown Chicago yesterday, was he?"

Her father's expression showed one of great concern. If it could talk, it might have said: *I saw a non-sanctioned parade that killed fifteen people and forced a woman to give premature birth in the back of a 1975 Mellow Yellow AMC Gremlin. That child will never be "normal."*

"What?" asked Addy, feigning ignorance. "I ... don't *think* so."

Her father looked old.

"Well, kiddo," he announced in a most parental fashion, "if you *are* ever asked to the prom, I say you just go. Right? As for now, I have to head into the kitchen to consume mass-produced, butter-substitute-soaked danishes. It's a new client. Just remember: The dreams you have as a kid don't always hold true. Did I ever think I'd be financially supporting a transfer student named Caedmon Chovanec?"

"Chonger," corrected Addy.

"I don't know," said her father.

"Being a teenager is the best years of one's life, huh?" joked Addy.

"Walls come crashing down," her father muttered, distracted. "It's all about the slippage, kiddo. Mindless, pulsating waves of heartbreak. But it's not all bad. I finally figured out how to fix that ad campaign for Wendy's. I hired a very old and ugly woman. So that's fun."

Her father appeared to be descending—more accurately *spelunking*—toward a burbling cauldron of infinite sadness.

But it was a *good* talk. Addy felt a whole lot better. Her father wasn't so bad after all, even if he did have an annoying tendency to hover over his children in putter-tattered cotton bathrobes and complain about adult depression to those far too young to ever understand or care about such matters.

He was like any other adult, Addy supposed. Just a simple man with modest dreams and humble aspirations. In his particular case, to die a gentle, leisurely death within an assisted care facility overlooking a Chi-Chi's just outside of town, with Medicare paying for it all.

Heaven.

Sometimes Addy wished she could stay a little girl forever. Or until she could afford her own apartment adjacent to the mall and get the hell out of here with an assistant manager's job at a store that featured some type of lame pun. But if she *had* to be stuck with parents, she supposed she could do a whole lot worse.

Still on the couch and clutching the one pink Capezio Jazz shoe—furiously speckled with a stranger's bone matter—Addy coiled into a tight ball and prayed herself into a quick, dreamless sleep, worlds away from the never-ending, neoned-pink nightmare of her existence.

Eventually, it arrived: a most amazing temporary suicide.

CHAPTER EIGHT

The Secret

"Hooray!" screamed the excitable girl on the basketball court. "Everybody say '*hooooraaaaaay*'!!"

"Hooray," mumbled Addy. "Yay."

Yet another useless pep rally ...

Lucy, who was to Cass's left, said not a word, merely staring off into space.

Kristina was checking her Maybelline Long-Wearing Nail Color polish on her fingernails. Under her breath, she sang, "Wear it classy, wear it sassy, wear it soft, wear it sleek, wear it light, wear it luscious ... wear it *long*."

From the gymnasium's floor came this pronouncement:

"IT IS TIME TO ROCK OUT FOR THE NORTHRIDGE HIGH PEP SQUAD! THE NORTHRIDGE LAZERS! WE ARE GOING TO BEAT THE BULLDOGS!! SO LET'S START THIS PART-TAY!!!"

Addy's psyche hurt like it did whenever she was painfully bored. She would have rather been anywhere else than right here, sitting in the stands, faking her enthusiasm.

How she wished she could just be alone at her desk, in her bedroom, with a fresh piece of paper and a giant pen with four different colors, repeatedly signing Roland's name over and over and over again, in loopy, moony, love-sick cursive ...

The rest of the Lazers bounded out. Addy noticed that one of them was Camilla, the short brunette she had met at Roland's party. She appeared very *bouncy*.

Addy didn't remember the last time she herself had bounded or bounced. Maybe it was at sketch night at summer camp when she was Grizabella from *Cats*? She had played the role "method style" as an *authentic* cat, leaping up on to the stage, urinating on a bedspread, hissing, and then bounding off the stage, never to return.

The Lazers were now forming a long line and all of the girls collectively began a cheer that rhymed "Northridge" with "Kill."

Rhyming was obviously not their specialty.

"How was the party?" whispered Grimer, sitting next to Addy. "You haven't said a word about it!" He scratched his forehead, just beneath his hat—nothing more than a spaghetti colander stolen from the cafeteria, cocked jauntily to the side.

It was dramatic and impractical and Addy loved it.

"Awful," replied Addy. "It wasn't *anything* I was hoping for. I'm so *disappointed*, Grimer."

"What were you expecting?" Grimer asked. "I mean, come on! You travel that far north, nothing good can come from it! It's like when I drove up to Milwaukee for the Hands Across America, only to return missing a kidney."

"But that *house*, Grimer!" said Addy. "*It was way beyond gorge in the most supreme*. The bathroom practically had its own bathroom! *Total scrote to the maxy-paddiest of the gladdiest!*"

"Meaning?"

"It's *Ramba* talk, okay? The house was *huge*! As large as Graceland! At least ten percent bigger than *my* shithole that's southwest of the lake!"

"Okay, *okay*," said Grimer, shielding his face as if he were in a cafeteria fight with an imaginary floating creature with translucent wings, an image with which he was well-acquainted.

The pep band launched into a brassy, upbeat version of Gordon Lightfoot's ode to maritime disaster, "Wreck of the Edmund Fitzgerald."

Addy was sick of all this fake high school cheer. Typical meaningless pep bullshit! What next? Yet one more stupid, flute-driven version of Joy Division's "Isolation"?

On the gymnasium floor, the school's mascot, a wise and courageous Indian chief, slowly retreated. He had just scalped the head of Northwood's rival school's mascot, Shermer High's Jiggling Hobo.

The principal, Dr. Mulligan, stepped forward and took the mic.

"I would like to ask Henry Thompson to please leave the gym. He's the sophomore who nearly died last week by auto-erotic-asphyxiation, only to be saved by his step-mother. That's pretty embarrassing!" He paused, clearing his voice. "If you're not sure where you currently stand in our complicated societal hierarchy, please refer to the digital breakdown in my office!"

He glanced down at his notes. It was clear that he

had forgotten what he was about to say. He really hadn't been the same since last spring's "senior prank," in which both of his ears had been ripped off by snickering seniors while he napped.

"I'd like to extend a fierce and spirited Injun welcome to a very special guest …"

"Did Roland invite you to the prom?" Grimer whispered to Addy.

"No," Addy replied. "He wanted to *kiss* me. But I said N-O."

"Playing hard to get," said Grimer, grinning, relieved. "I like that. You ain't making it easy for that Well-Heeled Flushy!"

Addy cringed at that *ain't*. So south of the lake. So 1981.

On the gym's floor, a middle-aged man took the microphone from Dr. Mulligan. "I'd like to thank all of you for having me today. My name is Todd. I'm back for the reunion, class of '53. And I'm here to give you some life advice. *Real* life advice. Not the fake kind. So let's get started. Never marry a woman with a tattoo on her forehead...."

"*Whaaaaaaa* …" fake cried Grimer. "*My wife has a tattoo on her forehead*!"

Addy laughed. Grimer really did make Addy giggle harder than anyone! That was just a fact.

But there were other facts: Grimer wasn't anywhere *close* to being as attractive as Roland. Or as rich. *'Cause the boy with the cold hard cash tended to be Mister Right.* That was *also* a fact. Where had Addy first heard that? An Emily Dickinson poem?

Regardless, it was the difference between a championship show dog with a satin blue ribbon attached to its leather collar and a lovable rescue mutt with two mangy testicles.

Sure, both were great but one was ... even *greater*.

Addy thought of Anne Frank again, and everything the girl had to go through.

But Anne Frank had only one boy choice to make: Peter.

Addy had *two* choices: Grimer or Roland.

What Addy was going through was *far* worse.

"Let's get the hell out of here," announced Kristina, bored of drawing a Magic Marker heart on her knee through her torn jeans. "Head over to the mall's food court for some inoffensive ethnic food."

"Yeah," said Cass. "Have you guys heard about the Blackened Everything? It's a Cajun-themed restaurant that burns everything to a carcinogenic, spicy, faddish deliciousness!"

"But if we leave now," said Addy weakly, eyeing the crowd, "they'll only laugh at us."

"Let 'em," said Kristina, walking quickly, nearly running, down the stands. She stepped on a few hands and laps but did not care. The rest of the gang followed. One seated Richie screamed, "Ouchy!" in a dramatic fashion as Danielle passed by.

"Goth go *bye-bye*," he said, as his friends laughed. He was wearing a T-shirt that read "My Other Ride is Your Mom."

Danielle shot him a look. *How many more years would she be stuck with these idiots?* She kept moving.

When they at last exited the gym, Kristina exclaimed, "God! That was more dull than Garfield overeating lasagna!"

Lucy grimaced. Personally, she found Garfield to be extraordinarily funny. Especially when he suffered from horrendous gas after consuming lasagna—just as she did. Among the many things they had in common— besides a terrific sense of humor—was lactose-intolerance.

Grimer took a step forward, opened his mouth, but said nothing. It was almost as if he had a huge announcement to make but was too scared to make it.

"Do you guys want to see something?" he finally asked, more than a bit nervous.

"And what would that be?" asked Lucy.

"Where I live," answered Grimer.

Kristina said: "I thought we were all going to the mall!"

"Come," said Grimer. "No more big questions."

Lucy was perplexed. There had only been one question, and a minor one at that.

Grimer made his way down Hallway B and then took a left into a connecting hallway. He hung a right into Hallway A and then walked straight into the library. The rest of the group followed.

"The *library*?" said Addy, disappointed. "I *hate* this place."

"Follow," said Grimer, walking straight past Mrs. Murray, the librarian for over thirty years, who was filling out a *TV Guide* crossword in *pen*—she was *that* bright—past the magazine rack stocked with *Ranger*

Rick and *Grit* and *Reverend Sun Myung Moon's Unification Church's Monthly*, and a few other exceedingly important periodicals, then past the "Quiet Area for Budding Depressives," past a group of five students, all from different a clique, but all from the same racial and socioeconomic makeup, endlessly chatting about something or other that was totally meaningless, these five never shut up, one was a richie red head, the other a jock, the other a nerd, the other a whatever, and then, finally into a FICTION aisle, directly between the RA – SO and the SU – TA stacks.

Grimer at last came to a stop.

"Where now?" asked Kristina. "We can't go any further."

Farther, thought Danielle.

"Are you ready to make the leap?" asked Grimer, mysteriously. "There's *no* going back."

"A leap into the wall?" asked Addy. "Where *exactly* are we leaping?"

Kristina, Danielle and Lucy looked at each other. They didn't know Grimer nearly as well as Addy did. Was this freak dangerous? Or just innocently insane?

Grimer crouched and pointed to a space just above the ancient carpeted floor. It was a hole in the brick wall covered with a piece of plywood. Addy had never noticed it before. Grimer removed it gently.

And then, much to Addy's and the others' astonishment, Grimer crawled directly through, straight into darkness.

Addy blinked. This reminded her of one of the waking dreams she'd experience every few months involving that Bigfoot-type creature who sat at the edge of her bed and innocently picked his nose.

But maybe this was even *more* scary.

Addy crouched just as Grimer had. She peeked into the entrance. Little could be seen but it didn't appear unsafe. She could always trust Grimer.

Right?

Oh, what the hell, she thought.

"Are we in?" she asked, turning back to her friends. They nodded.

Good. She wasn't in the mood for spicy, blackened, carcinogenic Cajun food this afternoon anyway.

Addy kneeled and crawled all the way through. The rest of the "Hang Gang" followed.

Once inside, they stood, brushing the dust off their pants.

Lucy declared, "It's almost as if we're descending into an ant's colony and headed straight into the queen's chamber!"

Grimer was already a few yards up ahead. He was making his way along a very narrow path located just next to the wall.

"Replace the plywood," he called back.

Addy caught up quickly, not wanting to be left behind. There was a strange beauty to it all. Addy could hear the muffled voices of students but she could not see them. She must have now been walking next to, or very close to, the gymnasium.

To Addy, it felt as if she were falling asleep in the afternoon on a hot summer's day, listening to the kids outside play and leap off houses without helmets.

Woozy waves of sound. A constant hum emanating from some very deep space within the inner cavity of the school; the depleted whirl of a huge fan. Tranquil core. Honeyed warmth.

The spaghetti colander on Grimer's head sparkled each time he passed a single-hanging light bulb.

The double-alarm sounded.

The pep rally, as horrible as it had been, was over. Time for class.

Not for Addy and the rest of the Hang Gang.

They walked on. If Grimer trusted Addy enough to show her his secret world, she could at least follow. Over wires, beneath pipes, an X-ray version of the hallways and classrooms Addy was so familiar with on the outside.

Grimer turned another corner and walked down yet another narrow passageway.

And it was here that he, at last, stopped.

"Are you ready to enter the world *within* the world?" he asked. He was standing before a small doorway.

Addy kind of wished he'd stop being so dramatic. This was cool but it wasn't *that* cool. She was just happy to be skipping her "Chicago Lake-Area Geography" honors class. "Sure," she answered.

"My home," Grimer grandly announced, walking into a large room. *"Welcome to my household!"*

When Addy would later look back on this moment, what she would most clearly remember—more than anything, even beyond the smell or even beyond Cass fainting and being revived with a bottle of industrial grade ammonia—was the string of Christmas lights

95

awkwardly hanging across the ceiling of this large room, blinking on again, off again, red, green, red, green.

Until Grimer eventually hit the overhead light switch and Addy saw what lay before her, the room reminded her of a wet stretch of nighttime road, reflecting street-lights, rhythmically beating in steady time, over and over and over, endlessly.

"It's not much," said Grimer. "But it is home. C'mere. I'll show you around."

The room was bigger than any classroom Addy had ever seen. It was cavernous.

Addy saw couches that Grimer must have stolen from the teacher's lounge. Addy saw throw rugs. Desks. A huge TV on a stand. Lamps. Tables. A CPR manne-quin leaning against a brick wall wearing a "JUST SAY NO!" T-shirt.

"An old band room, in a forgotten wing, bricked over," explained Grimer. "Hasn't been used in years. Notice all the instruments?"

Addy did. There was a piano in one corner. Against the opposite wall, two kettle drums sat with a canopy strung across the tops. A small mattress lay on the ground between the timpanis.

There was a soda machine that must have been stolen from one of the hallways and that only dispensed cans of Mello Yello. Addy knew that just last year the Repub-lican-run USDA had enthusiastically credited the drink with meeting the daily nutritional fruit requirements for a nourishing child's breakfast.

"My god," said Lucy.

"It's like a nightmare," said Danielle, happily.

"Cooler than the mall," said Lucy without thinking, and then hurriedly crossed herself. *Where had such a terrible thought ever come from?*

Besides the instruments, Addy noticed all of the ropes, the pulleys, the gears. Everything seemingly connected to *something*.

She had to give Grimer at least some credit for building a living space that reminded her of something the Swiss Family Robinson would have built if they, too, had somehow washed up inside a suburban high school and had zero taste and no access to bamboo or coconuts.

Grimer pulled a rope, which somehow turned on a portable stereo, or "jam box." A song could be heard. It was by one of Addy's favorite groups, Soft Cell.

Addy had a huge crush on the Cell's lead singer, Marc Almond. But sadly, and last she read in *Teen Wanc*, Marc was already seriously involved with a very special, beautiful adult woman.

Sigh. It was always the male singers who wore the best Flame-Go lipstick who were the least available ...

"This is where I sleep," said Grimer, proudly, pointing to a spot between the kettle drums.

"Wha—?" began Addy.

She was at a total loss. She had no idea where to even begin. Neither did Kristina, who was *never* at a loss for something to say, except occasionally with her "sexual safe word."

But Addy figured this to be as good a start as any: "How ... how long have you lived here, Grimer? You actually live *inside* the school?"

"I think you should all have a seat," answered Grimer.

"This might, um, take awhile."

They did as they were told.

CHAPTER NINE

Grimer's Story

"Just let me get through the entire story, okay?" said Grimer, sitting in a chair, across from Addy and the rest who were reclining on a cracked-leather lounge couch.

Grimer took a deep breath, steadying himself for the story of a lifetime, one that could last for hours. And he let loose:

"I never knew my mother. Or father. When my mom was eighteen—a senior here at this school—she gave birth in the first floor bathroom. She headed back to the prom, abandoning me. A kind-hearted security guard heard me crying and rescued me. He raised me right here, within this building. Sadly, he died ten years ago, leaving me all alone."

Addy was entranced. *Wow! What a story!*

She waited for whatever could possibly be coming next.

She couldn't imagine where this story might be headed!

"That's it," Grimer finished.

"That's it?" asked Lucy.

"That's the entire story?" asked Danielle, surprised.

Addy blinked. Truthfully, she had expected a much better ending, but she had to admit that what Grimer had managed to say in that last half minute had certainly packed a punch.

"So you grew up *in* school?" asked Kristina. "Like Tarzan in jungle?"

Kristina was so excited she wasn't even using the word "the," almost like the real Tarzan himself.

"What did you survive on?" asked Addy. "What did you eat?"

"Same food as now. Frozen items from the cafeteria. Fruit roll-ups. Capri Sun. Sandwiches. All the foods that people who wear retainers throw away."

"How do you earn money to survive?" asked Cass.

"I need so very little. But I sell frozen tater tots to old age homes and hospices," responded Grimer, pointing to a stack of boxes in the corner that reached as high as the ceiling. "They'll buy *anything*. I also sell ACT test answers."

Lucy laughed. "I always wondered how this school became the highest-ranked academic institution in the world!" she said.

"Where do you shower and clean yourself?" asked Kristina.

"Not often."

"Right. But *where*?" Addy asked.

"The showers in the girls' locker room. Really, Addy. This place has everything I need. A working bathroom over there," he pointed, "and even a hot plate. I never even have to leave this room. It's super cozy. It's not that complicated."

Addy looked around. This room—this *home*—did seem rather cozy. And clever. The inventions were the product of a smart mind.

Addy typically hated *function* over *appearance*. But not in this case.

"Come on," said Grimer. "I want to show you all something."

Grimer led the girls over to a corner that was filled with canvases and cans of paints and even an easel. There was an endless supply of pens, brushes, ink bottles, all no doubt stolen from art classrooms. "This is where I do my drawing and painting. Can I show you some?"

Grimer lifted a sheet revealing a stack of artwork.

Addy was stunned. Each of the pieces was gorgeous. Delicate paintings and superb line-drawings of students and teachers, each so exceedingly detailed, all practically resembling photographs.

"These are ... *incredible*, Grimer," Addy announced, meaning it.

"I really like the nude ones," said Lucy, pointing to an illustration of Mrs. Wilkins, the sixty-five-year-old gym teacher, holding two flesh-colored tube socks with weighted ends in front of her chest.

The socks practically came down to her waist.

Lucy looked closer. *Wait. Those weren't socks ...*

Grimer blushed and adjusted his colander. "I want to get into the arts. Draw and paint. That is if I ever get out of here. I so want to escape one day. I have to be honest. I debated for a long, long time on whether to show you any of this. I just thought now was as good a time as any. And I was hoping this wouldn't ruin our friendships ..."

"Hey, Yoid! Thirsty?!"

"Baby doll. You've been reading too many Harlequin romances. Dip your red locks into some of my reality!"

"Are we done here? I have to go over to the stables and comb out the horse."

Addy dressing for Halloween as Dustin Hoffman in Tootsie

"I wrote you a love poem: 'If you were to lick my heart, you'd die from the poison' . . . ."

The powerful "ghetto jam box"

The high-tech computer screen in which Addy "communicates" with Roland.

A poster from the Bedroom Wall Poster Outlet, a store that specializes in less popular posters for girls

The Yarnkin creature that Addy simply adores

A poster from the Bedroom Wall Poster Outlet, a store that specializes in less popular posters for girls

A preppie with his "stink finger" extended all fancy like, just so!

"I want you to really accentuate 'Eat Dirt,' almost as if it's your first time. Say it. Slower. Faster. Again. Concentrate!"

Annette the "punker" shows us that what's good for the geese is always good for the gander!

Grimer and Addy joined at the "unhip"

"When you silently mouth 'die,' there's a look in your eyes. I can't explain it. I just have to see it. Do it again. Take two hundred and forty-seven!"

Danielle's goth boyfriend Bingo before he dies in a farming accident.

ROLAND: "I'm so sorry that my entire family despises you for your lack of wealth."

ADDY: "That's okay. Don't talk. You're gorgeous."

Sludge, Kaitlyn's 57-year-old hydrocephalic bo!

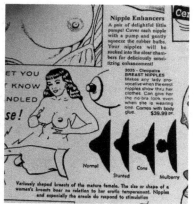

Addy's unfortunate "mulberry" shaped nipple

"Hahahahaha! Ha! Ha! Oh my god!!!!!!"

"To hell with the Lake fancies!"

"I wasn't the one who called. It was Chonger. The China transfer student."

"No condom, no yum yum!"

"I made you that mixed tape I promised. Do you adore Huey Lewis played for 90 minutes straight?"

Meet Choad! He's as rock and roll as it gets . . . and then some!

"Get out of my room, Justin, before I tell momma 'bout the rubber vagina!"

Grimer and Addy at the . . . where else? The Mall!

"Kaitlyn, you're only a few years older than me but you look so much wiser. For a reason! Because you've had loads of the sex!"

Gother don't care!

"Does this really go with my helmet?"

"So much style, grace and debonair for one young man!"

Tina, Platty and Gill!

"Come with me to the poor section. I want to show you the Electric Salamander!"

Sally from the Unicorned Rainbow. She's a "hoot"!

"Addy! You promised!"

Uh oh! The Grimer "cuts up"!

If there's grass on the field, play ball!

Virgins hunger for some of that fresh 'tang. Yeah!
They like dat!

"Say deep dish pizza cheeeeeeeeeeeeeese!'"

Addy and Kaitlyn, the Titty Committee. Uh oh! Looks like two "members" didn't show!

"Girl, I smell you!"

Warriors in that most dangerous game known to man . . . "High School."

Even "New Wavers" can get hungry and feel the "urge" to hit the mall's
incredible food court!

"There's only five months left until prom. *Really* show your hurt."

Addy raises $73 for the freshman still in a coma from the horrific
Benihana grill incident!

"Grimer, you stink like holy hell and you are as ugly as a slide-trombon-
ist in an all-white ska band, but you DO make me laugh!"

"Move, Yoid!"

[Outtake, did not make "final cut"]

"Magic time" in remedial sex ed

Moments before Grimer barfs and suffers the mysterious day-long seizure

Vroom vroom! Gotta keep those engines runnin' "clean"!

Before the Sadie Hawkins dance and after the donkey basketball championship in which Northridge loses terribly and the Jiggling Hobo dies

"Of course not!" exclaimed Addy. "Grimer, we love you as a friend. Or at least I do. You're a good person. And you're intelligent. At least I think you are. *Maybe*. You know things about me that no one else in the world knows!"

"Yes," said Grimer. "For a *reason*. I have a vantage point no one else in the school has. I'm all-seeing, all-hearing. Like a god."

To Addy, this sounded a bit egotistical. She personally didn't believe in religion or gods.

She only believed in vibrant, saturated colors and the thirty minutes each week MTV played "alternative" music.

"Meaning what?" Addy asked.

"Meaning," explained Grimer, "that I'm able to spy on people. I'm able to watch history from above. The *best* perspective."

"And that's how you know stuff about me?" Addy asked.

Grimer nodded.

"What do you know about *me*?" asked Kristina.

"I know you fall asleep in home ec," said Grimer.

"And me?" asked Danielle.

"I know you secretly listen to old jazz standard LPs in the library," said Grimer.

Danielle blushed and fiddled with her brand new, freshly ironed Bauhaus T-shirt.

"And me?" asked Lucy, finally.

"Yeah, um …" said Grimer. He left it at that.

"How do you do it?" Addy asked, a tad defensively. "You know, spy on us?"

"I can show all of you," said Grimer. "If you're interested. I mean, eventually."

They nodded. It was a sort of dream come true. *To become the eyes and ears of the entire school!*

"Like observing an ant farm!" said Lucy, excitedly. "I feel as powerful as my pet mantis Miss Verde!"

"Wait a second," said Addy. There was a look of concentration on her face. "Wait a second here ..."

She was thinking.

"Yes," said Grimer, thrilled and relieved to at last be sharing this very special secret that he had been keeping to himself for so very long. "What is it?"

"Well, listen," Addy said. "So ... are you telling me that I will learn things about Roland McDough that I wouldn't have known otherwise? Is that what you're telling me?"

The Hang Gang looked at each other and rolled their eyes. *Here we go ...*

Grimer looked confused. "No. But I guess you *could* learn a few things about him. If you wanted."

Addy grew even more excited. "And are you telling me that I can spy on Roland to learn exactly what he's looking for in a woman?"

"No," said Grimer, looking even more deflated. "But again ..."

"Would that even be right?" continued Addy. "Wouldn't that be sort of like cheating?"

Roland shrugged. "Probably. I guess. I don't know. But I'm here to help if you decide you want to. Especially if the alternative is you telling the authorities on me."

The two came together to hug. Addy recoiled quickly from the fecund Earthy odor that reminded her of that car crash from the other night. Feral or not, Grimer stunk.

More than that, Addy noticed that the hug was more passive-aggressive than was typical. It was almost as if Grimer was still a tad jealous of Roland.

Addy knew there was a Passive-Aggressive Hug Club in the school for squealing girls who liked to pretend they were happy for the success of other squealing girls—if one, say, had made the Pep Squad and the other hadn't—but Addy had never attended a meeting.

Had Grimer spied on this club? And was he now emulating their disturbing methods?

"Thank you, Grimer!" said Addy, finally. "I would *love* to do that!"

Grimer went to high-five Addy, who purposely missed. The kid smelled like death on crackers.

"You know, Grimes," Addy laughed, "I'm only now starting to understand your incredible bizarreness. It's all beginning to make sense. It's that feeling I always get when talking to you that you're not quite fully baked. A tad unhinged."

Such a statement might have been construed by most people as "rude," especially if that certain someone had raised himself as an undomesticated creature within a public high school and was capable of doing god knows what within the bizarre reality of his own curious upbringing.

But Grimer didn't seem to mind.

"How about grades?" asked Kristina. "Could you improve ours for us?"

"I can, yes," said Grimer. "I can easily hack into the computers. That's what I do for myself."

Everyone except Lucy smiled. *She would earn her grades the old-fashioned way, thank you very much! By not leaving her bedroom until she had a headache and was nauseated from memorizing useless equations and formulas.*

But for all of them, they had just crossed some sort of line.

After learning Grimer's secrets and hidden abilities, there was no going back, not for this group.

"How do I get back?" Addy asked, suddenly.

"There's no going back," said Grimer, seriously.

"No, seriously. How do I get back?" Lucy asked, a bit panicked. "I have to return to sulking in the hallways."

Grimer showed her, and the rest, the way.

CHAPTER TEN

A New and Improved Addy

Things were looking up.

And not only because of the discovery of Grimer's secret Back World the previous week.

The night before, Addy had sat down with her father while he was sipping Sanka from a cracked NUMBER #1 DAD mug that he had purchased during a PBS fundraising segment featuring America's very own "Number One Dad," Bill Cosby.

After taking a bite of his margarine-drenched snack, her father had said: "Addy, you're valuable; a *commodity*. No different than any product I market. Do you remember when I worked on that New Coke endeavor? Or NASA after the Challenger explosion? Or after IHOP changed their name to IHOS: 'International House of Sadness'? You're basically the same: a bit of a disaster but not yet worth dumping."

"So what do I do?" Addy had asked, flattered.

"Simple," her father had answered. "Re-brand!"

Addy had to admit that her dad was on to something. Depressing and horrible to be around, but mostly correct.

Entenmann's Raspberry Danish Twist crumbs tickling his bare chest, her father went on: "You're only as good as people are *told* you are. And that's a wonderful thing, Addy! A very American thing! Just tell 'em you're *great*! End of story! Simple!"

"But why would they believe me, daddy?" she had asked.

"Americans believe anything they're told. Unless Democrats are saying it," he had answered. "Just flesh the message. Re-spin the image. Come up with a new name for yourself."

"Different than 'Addy'?"

"Add 'New and Improved'," he had said. "Same amazing personality, brand-new look. Find out what the people *want*. And then just *give* it to them. *Ta-da*."

Addy had nodded and kissed her father on his cheek.

She then rushed upstairs to slow dance with Yarnkin to "Mad World" by Tears for Fears.

The next morning, at quarter past eight, Addy entered into the Secret World via a small entrance beneath the water fountain in Hallway C.

Grimer was already there to welcome her.

They had so much to do.

The cut-off date in which Roland could invite Addy to the prom before it became embarrassing was quickly approaching.

The digital sign in the principal's office counted down the hours, minutes, seconds.

No one ever questioned the digital board.

"Where do we start?" asked Addy.

Grimer looked down at a computer printout. "Roland's first class appears to be Just Enough French to Cheat with Your Future Au Pair."

"Then let's go!" exclaimed Addy.

Holding his flashlight and walking confidently down a narrow interior path on the east side of the school, Grimer led Addy across the water pipes, up a rope ladder, and then to a spot above a classroom, where he took a prone position, peering down. He motioned for Addy to come over: "*This* way. The best position to watch Roland!"

Addy kneeled and peered through a small hole in the perforated ceiling.

Addy could clearly see Roland, beneath her, sprawled coquettishly. He looked to have brought his own special rocking chair from home. On the back, in fancy cursive, it read: *Le Roland.*

"See anything?" Grimer asked from behind her.

"All that I need to," answered Addy.

"How about *hear*?" whispered Grimer. "Can you hear anything?"

"Shhhh," said Addy. "Let me *listen.*" She placed her ear to the ceiling's hole and caught a snippet of conversation. It was Roland's voice:

"I love it when girls dress just like me, you know? I hate it when they have their own *style.*"

He accentuated the word *style* to make it sound very funny, similar to Mr. T on the *A-Team* when he was fake angry. It was the only black person Roland knew ... and he pitied the fool who didn't also know at least one!

"What's he saying?" asked Grimer, from behind Addy. "C'mon, Addy!"

Addy whispered: "He's saying that he likes a woman ... with great confidence ... a smart woman, with a personality ... and ... one he can easily manipulate ...

126

into something they're ... not ..."

Addy had heard all this before. This very scenario had played itself out a few years before to a beautiful Australian transfer student named Sandy and her idiot, fey, greaser boyfriend named Danny who was the leader of a gang called ... Addy couldn't remember. The Chuff Nuts? Regardless, their relationship had ultimately ended horribly: a murder/suicide as doo-wop blasted over carnival speakers.

But that wasn't even the worst case. A few years after *that* event, something even more *devastating* occurred:

An athletic type—he looked to be some sort of doughy wrestler—had somehow convinced an introverted, goth outcast prone to black outfits and shaking dandruff "snow" onto drawings to fix herself up real nice. They started dating and ultimately married. They moved into a three-bedroom ranch house on the outskirts of Detroit.

Currently, they're not *unhappy*, per se. Both are still alive and in good health. But they're also just sort of confused as to what they first found attractive about each other to begin with. More sad and numb than anything else. It just all seems so *goddamned* long ago.

Addy shivered. *God forbid anything like that should ever happen to her.*

"I think we have our answer," Addy said, turning to Grimer.

"What?" asked Grimer, confused. "What answer?"

"It's *makeover time*!" whispered Addy, confidently. "Time for a major re-brand!"

Grimer smiled weakly.

"Come on!" whispered Addy. "We must get Roland to notice me again. Just exactly how he wants me to look. There's no time to waste!"

Actually, there was.

Plenty.

Addy often felt as if time were dipped into amber and she was only moving 16 rpm in a 45 rpm world. So … slow. Life just moved so … *slowly*.

It felt again like that summer between the seventh and eighth grades, when Addy cheered on Stuey, the neighborhood idiot, as he attempted—*endlessly, without rest*—to throw Frisbees through the moon. That summer lasted for seemingly generations.

The passage of time was a strange thing.

Has anyone ever written a poem about it? Addy thought. *If not, someone definitely should!*

But now … time actually seemed to be speeding up a bit, which Addy didn't mind at all.

Let's get this thing called "life" on the road!

With Grimer leading the way, Addy climbed down from the top of Roland's French class and began the next stage of her rapidly improving life.

To celebrate, she popped on a pair of miniature cassette Walkman's feather-light headphones—*light in scale, formal in feeling*—and began listening to one of her favorite new *alterna* songs.

The song was called "Kissing the Pink," and it was almost as if it had been written especially for her. She sang along as she walked through the semi-darkness:

She was a different type of girl,

From the colored part of town.
But the only color that mattered ...
Was pink for her prom gown.

Kissing the pink!
She's not like the others.
Colors outside the box, a whole different breed!
Kissing the pink!
She got the colors I want now,
she got the colors I need now ...
I need to be kissing that pink!

Girl, I got the colors you're seeking,
Blue moon in the evening, white satin at night.
Step into my gray car now,
Feel my temporary rainbow grow tight.
Girl, save my color sample, it's yours for the
taking.
Think over my offer but please only tell me "yes."
And when you've made up your mind now,
I'll slip off your real pink prom dress.

You know you want it.
You know you need it.
You gotta kiss that pink ...
You just gotta kiss that pink.

CHAPTER ELEVEN

Hi, Hi, Hi

It was "flex" time, that fifteen-minute gap at the peak of the school day, the free period in which students could do whatever they wished, be it study or chat or have a languid, leisurely smoke in the designated area in the rear of the van owned by the math substitute, Mister Johnson.

Mister Johnson, otherwise known as "Mister Jay," was a really cool teacher who'd allow any of the boys to play his home videogame system—Commodore Executive 64—back at his one-bedroom apartment off the highway access road. In return, Mister Johnson only asked for a twenty-minute "back gruzzle."

Roland was now making long, multiple loops around and around the first floor hallways, staring at his own reflection whenever he passed a glass trophy case.

Roland loved champions but he did not believe in athletic sweat. He only preferred to sweat—*if at all*—when he was in the thick of some serious solo primping. Or when he was on the slunky, funky move, as he was now, down along the corridor of Hallway A.

His outfit was most supreme: white Izod (one button still missing), a brown and suede blazer, thick, comfory cords, lambswool driving cap, and mirrored contacts.

Students, even teachers, were observing Roland, just as Roland always knew they were.

Ramba style.

Roland casually nodded to a fellow Richie he recognized from their country club, Restricted Pines, and went to turn the corner—

And ... *Addy was right there, in front of him, like a thriftshop-wearing apparition.*

"Oh my velvet word!" exclaimed Roland. "I ... I've been trying to call you! How are you? You left the party so ... *rapidly*. I was so very concerned!"

Addy smiled. She knew Roland was lying. She had not received any such message.

"I talked with your mother," Roland continued. "Did she not tell you I called? I'm surprised."

On second thought, maybe Roland wasn't lying after all. Addy's mother—especially when bubbling off the goofy gumbo—had a tendency to ... forget any and all messages. Whether they had been delivered in reality or not ...

Typically, her mother would fall asleep each night, drunk, on the couch, with a book on top of her face. It was always the same book: *Cool Ways to Talk with Your Difficult Daughter! How to Relate the <u>New</u> Old Fashioned Way!*

Phone calls typically had a way of going unanswered.

"If you *did* call," declared Addy, nicer than she had any right to be, "I didn't get the message. I'm sorry. I didn't mean to leave so quickly from the party. I was ... *uncomfortable*. Outside my groan zone."

"I understand, Addy. I just want to apologize for

what happened. My friends are nothing more than idiots whenever their stupidity is mocked in front of others who are a lot smarter."

Addy attempted to decipher the nuances of this statement but she quickly gave up. It just wasn't worth it. On the other hands, *those eyes* ...

"Perhaps," said Addy, non-committedly. She was playing it super smooth. "Anyway, I wasn't very happy with what I saw you doing with Chonger. No foreigner should ever be used as a sex-game bottle. We'll talk. *Maybe*."

Addy walked around Roland and continued down the hallway, towards her locker.

Roland looked after her. And then continued on his way, passing the classroom for the "A.V. Clubbers."

The Clubbers always made a wonderful show of hooting and hollering whenever Roland strolled past. His physical perfection sexually stimulated them, especially the girl in the wheelchair with the pirate flag attached to the back. It was the highlight of their day, as it was Roland's, even topping the half-assed kiss that was blown his way by the attendance secretary each morning after he arrived a few hours late.

Roland turned his head to the side, readying himself to wave and wink—

And ... *Addy was suddenly in front of him again!*

"Addy!" he exclaimed. "*Weren't you*—didn't I just see you headed in the *opposite* direction?"

Addy shrugged. She kept on walking.

This was strange.

Roland was not particularly "proficient" at piecing

together an event that seemed contrary to what he was expecting—he'd leave that to those who earned less money and who worked with their hands while wearing heavy-soled workboots—but even to his untrained mind, something *really* wasn't right here.

Roland watched as Addy wended her way ahead through the crowded hallway. There she went, her bright red hair so easy to make out, so stark against the rest of the other kids' hair, just bobbing along like a bad simile in a sea of something or other whatchamacallit.

Roland headed for Hallway B—he'd always had fantastic luck in Hallway B, especially when it came to earning the attention of the Super Major League Dorks, or, as he often called them, "The Lessers"—but, just as he rounded the corner, Addy again came walking towards him.

Roland was confused. Which only made him incensed. Which only made him more confused. Which only made him more incensed.

What in the hell was going on here?

Roland increased his pace. He would walk straight into Hallway C, a place he had never even dared to trek. And if Addy was there, well ... *he didn't know what.*

He turned the corner. More unfamiliar faces. Were these even students? A few carried musical instruments. A few had the unmitigated gall to wear *non*-designer lazy-eye patches.

This place—Hallway C—was far, far worse than any of the urban legends!

Roland recognized some students he had only heard about through the years but had never actually seen: the kid who discovered a severed ear in an abandoned lot and kept it in his locker. The kid who forced his autistic brother to count cards in Vegas. The student caught "Judy Blumeing" herself in the first floor bathroom.

The principal, Dr. Mulligan, didn't even bother listing these losers on his digital board.

Addy didn't seem to be anywhere close to this hallway. Roland relaxed a bit but still quickened his step. *Best not to take a chance. He didn't know what he'd do if he were to see her again. Just a few more minutes and Flex period will end and he'd be able to relax in class in his rocking chair ...*

"Hey, Butler," said Roland, passing a fellow senior, someone he used to be friendly with in the eighth grade but stopped hanging out with after a horrible, year-long fight over who was the coolest Sweathog. "Sorry to hear about your mom dying."

"That was five years ago."

"Never heals," said Roland, entering his final lap. *This was fun!*

Making his way through these last moments of Flex period—a Richie among the plebes—always reminded Roland of how Paul McCartney and Stevie Wonder abolished racism forever with "Ebony and Ivory."

Like the both of them, Roland was quite possibly a hero.

And ... *Addy was coming towards him again.*

Roland stopped. *Huh?*

What exactly was happening here?!

Addy passed on his left.

This girl—this Addy Stevenson—*she was so myste-*

rious!

Strange, yes.

And a horrific dresser. The worst Roland had ever seen. And no fun at parties. She didn't drink. She didn't kiss. She didn't use drugs. She didn't make excruciating small talk about stocking fridges in third houses or purchasing vanity plates without vowels.

Regardless, there was something about this girl that was ... so very *intriguing*.

He'd have to think more about her.

True, she had greatly embarrassed him in front of his friends by acting all Yoid.

Unconscionable.

But it was also true that she was different from all the girls he knew. He shouldn't give up on her.

Not yet anyway.

Roland blinked back his designer mirrored contacts and made his way over to his next class: Business Accounting for Conservatives with Money.

Flex time was nearly over.

Behind the scenes, in the Back World, Addy and Grimer hugged.

Their mission had succeeded:

Roland had stood *zero* chance.

He was forced now to pay additional attention to Addy ... even if Addy continued to apparently give him the cold shoulder.

Which was just the way Addy wanted it.

Didn't all of the greatest romantic relationships in history—including Ronnie and Nancy's—begin this way? Time for step two ...

CHAPTER TWELVE

Musical Montage!

Was there any place on Earth better than the indoor shopping mall on a warm, beautiful early spring afternoon? Parisian street replications with overhead artificial stars. Glass elevators carrying passengers toting plastic-bags up and down, from the first to the second and then back to the first floor again, like a chariot of the gods. Sunken, moldy-carpeted rest areas abutting glorious miniature water falls, some chlorinated, most not.

Addy was with Grimer inside this indoor faux paradise, choosing the most *perfect* outfit to convince Roland that Addy was "The One"—the girl most willing to change her entire look, her entire essence, really anything you could think of and a few you couldn't—exclusively for him!

Which could only mean one thing: It was time for a full and complete physical "make over"!

Addy and Grimer had ignored the Non-Richie area of the mall entirely, and headed straight to the Richie Casherio section. So many stores Addy had never seen—let alone been in! It was almost like a musical montage one would see in a movie but made even *more* exciting because this was real life! And real life was *never* like this!

Addy within a fancy dressing room, doors flying open, pants flying out, all nearly hitting Grimer!

Addy posing in front of a triple-view mirror from so many different angles, a few from even above!

Grimer shaking his head "no" at the outfits, that's not quite the "one" ...

An older woman tsk-tsking Addy's stereotypical teenage behavior but secretly smiling; she used to be a teenager once!

Addy dancing, with her arms and legs flailing, putting on one new outfit after another, after another, every few seconds!

A certain advertising copywriter on his lunch break, eating a cheeseburger in the food court—just one burger, no one will see, what could it possibly do to his heart?—*who performs a theatrical doubletake when he sees a girl who looks exactly like his daughter, which is all but impossible, as she is still in school, she never skips!*

Addy choosing *this* item, choosing *that* item, Grimer still shaking his head, the workers rolling their eyes, *would this strange red-haired girl ever make a decision?, when would this all be over so we can re-fold the clothes?,* the workers sighing loudly. Addy balking at the ridiculous Richie price tags.

Grimer slipping a pair of pants on his head to make Addy laugh!

Grimer somersaulting down aisles, the security guards unable to control this savage suburban critter!

So much forced laughter, so much staged hilarity, until at last, with a sudden jarring stop, the montage comes to a screeching end—

And Addy and Grimer find themselves standing in front of the "Voluntary Subjugation" kiosk, just next to the Nipple-Piercing Kiosk, just next to the *Customize Anything!* store, in front of the *100% Authentic European "Gelato-Like" American Ice Cream* stand, down a ways from the store that only sells Pac Man-themed business attire, next to The Latest, a store that specializes in selling "the latest," no matter what it happens to be.

The pressure is tremendous. Even after three minutes, Addy and Grimer still have not found just that *perfect* outfit to convince Roland that Addy is *the one*—the girl most willing to change her entire look, her entire essence, exclusively for him.

Which is why the "Voluntary Subjugation" kiosk now seems so inviting.

"I love this ESPRIT tampon holder," Grimer says, handing over a pair to Addy. "The total opposite of the real you!"

"I thank you again for doing this, Grimer," says Addy. "I realize that you're still a tad jealous."

Grimer gives a tight smile.

In truth, he *is* still jealous of Addy's crush on Roland but he figures there's still plenty of time before the end of the school year to win her over.

"Who's the target?" the kiosk worker asls cheerfully.

"A Richie from the north side of the lake," answers Addy, with great pride.

"Then you'll definitely want this and this and this and *this*," says the worker, pulling down appropriate articles of clothing from the "Yoid to Richie" shelf, beginning with a black Croakie sunglass retainer to wear around her neck like any model from *Teen Wanc.*

"I love it!" says Addy, not knowing how to put it on.

"*Not* you in a nutshell," states Grimer. "When will the big reveal take place?"

"Tomorrow! Parking lot. After school."

"All you need now is an appropriate second-hand pin from Kristina!" says Grimer, looking on approvingly.

"I don't think so," Addy responds weakly, black Croakie retainer around her neck all wrong, jabbing her esophagus. "No *second-hand* for this girl anymore!"

The kiosk worker smiles. "That's the *new* fake you!"

Addy looks in the small mirror next to the register. Her new look is interesting.

Not just *good* good.

But *Ramba* good.

Addy motions to Grimer to pay the woman with his earnings from the stolen tater tots. She then she walks over to the Nipple-Piercing Kiosk, a few yards away.

Perhaps they have a clip-on option?

Another montage starts, this time with a different song, but with the same general principle.

CHAPTER THIRTEEN

The New Me!

Just like *that*, Addy was leaning against Roland's Karmann Ghia—color: Gentile Gray—in the student parking lot, waiting for Roland to exit the school, scratching absently at the rash caused by the clip-on nipple ring she wore for an hour after the mall and then discarded.

Addy had spent the morning in classes but the rest of the day in The Lair going over her game plan with Lucy, Danielle and Cass, which boiled down to Addy leaning against Roland's Karmann Ghia, in her new outfit, smack dab in the middle of the student parking lot, just waiting.

Not one of her friends necessarily *wanted* Addy to go out with Roland or to change her appearance in order to impress him, but would they have acted any differently in the same situation? If a Richie happened to be interested in *them*? Addy thought probably not.

When you were in love, there was *nothing* to be done. The heart wants what the hearts wants. Even if the brain desperately wants a phrase a little less cliché.

The last bell rang. From her position against the Karmann Ghia, Addy nodded to the students who were exiting the school, a few of whom held their gazes a little longer than was typical.

They were definitely noticing something new and super exciting about Addy ...

And if they did, Roland would, too!

Addy was kicking herself for not having made this transformation years ago. Life would have been so much *easier!*

Why work so hard at improving oneself when one can easily pay *to become what one is not?*

"Addy!"

Oh no!

That voice could only belong to one person—

It was her spastic spaz of a brother!

Justin approached, smiling of course, wearing a dorky *Space Skirmishes* or *Sky Scuffles* or *Star Problems* or whatever-the-hell-it-was-called themed backpack.

Space Shit.

That was it.

Addy hated that movie and all others like it. Too dark. Not enough neon. Not nearly enough teen angst. Way too many hucking and clucking space creatures with unwanted hair. Were there no razors or waxing supplies in space? Where exactly were all the *attractive* creatures who smelled nice? They should have focused on a Ramba planet in the northwest side of the north-ernmost end of the galaxy.

"Where's Chonger?" Addy asked her brother. She had not seen him since the party at Roland's house and feared that he now might be dead.

Justin removed his stereo cassette player headphones attached to his miniature, portable cassette player.

"What did you say?"

"I ask where Chonger go," said Addy, not knowing why she always spoke like this whenever referring to Chonger, just knowing it felt right.

"He's with his girlfriend," Justin said. "His *American* girlfriend."

"Chonger have American girlfriend?!"

"Yup," answered Justin. "Met at an impromptu breakdance battle on Interstate 90. She's a Richie. Speaking of which, what's with your new get up? You're looking all Richie yourself."

"That's the point, spaz!" declared Addy.

"But why?" asked Justin, genuinely puzzled. "I don't get it."

"You *wouldn't* get it," said Addy. "It's above your pay grade."

Justin shrugged and walked away, towards home, nonplussed, but still awkwardly smiling.

Even the phrase "above your pay grade" appeared to be above his pay grade. Addy felt sorry for him.

Totally oblivious to the nuances of the complicated popularity hierarchy of the high school!

Addy swiveled her body slightly against the car. She was starting to lose sensation in her lower extremities, which was fine. Fainting might even help her look *more* vulnerable when Roland did finally emerge—

And here he was now, strutting most smoothly from out of the school!

He was alone.

Good!

"What are you doing here?" Roland asked when he

at last reached her. "I mean, it's something else, you know? I've been running into you over and over again! It's so *strange*! I can't help but pay attention to you!"

"Huh?" answered Addy, pretending not to notice, staring at a particularly fascinating cloud pattern just above her, imagining what the clouds most closely resembled, finally deciding on Kevin Bacon's armpit stains in *Footloose*.

"Wow! You look ... *amazing*! Your outfit! It looks so *purchased*. What in the world has happened to you?"

"Is that good or bad?" Addy asked, a bit defensively.

"It's *good*!" said Roland. "Better than good! *Excellent* good!"

Addy relaxed. She was practically home free with this gorgeous north-of-the-lake idiot.

She waited for the inevitable: an invite to prom.

She'd been thinking about this moment for years, ever since watching Stephen King's *Carrie* on network TV. She would have to watch the unedited version on cable one day. Maybe that version ended happier.

"Would you ..." began Roland. "Addy, would you like—"

"Babe!" called out an approaching voice. "Babe!
Ugh!
The last thing Addy now needed!
Pribbenow!
The worst!
He was quickly approaching, wearing an untied silk kimono robe that featured a dragon sucking hard on a ceramic bong. One of his arms was draped confidently around his latest girlfriend, Jill Standish. The other was

holding an extendable 1930s cigarette holder.

"Well, well, well," triple-slimed Pribbenow. "Isn't this of a most *interesting* nature?"

"C'mon, Pribbs," said Roland, more upset than Addy had ever seen him. "Just me and a friend talking, that's all."

"About what?" asked Pribbenow. "Two lovebirds just chirp-chirp-*chirpin'* away?"

He took a dainty puff from his cigarette.

Roland sighed. "I was just about to ask Addy to the country club party."

You were? thought Addy.

"That should be most interesting," supercilioused Pribbenow, studying his fingernails carefully. "But will fancy country club chickies not recognize when a grimy street pigeon is in their midst?"

Jill Standish laughed heartily.

"Can grimy pigeons even fly?" continued Pribbenow, now cinching his kimono's sash. "Or do they just drag themselves from party to party on their diseased back legs?"

"Come on, man," said Roland. "Just lay off, okay?"

Pribbenow put his hands up, as if to defend himself. "Okay, babe. All right then. Have to *skedaddle* anyway! I'll see you both on the rebound. *Au Revoir.*"

Pribbenow made a big show of kissing his new girl-friend as they walked away. The sound reminded Addy of something you might hear from a dying manatee at SeaWorld.

As he passed, Pribbenow whispered in Addy's ear: "Girl, I *smell* you."

Was that a good thing?

"Alcohol you later!" he said to Roland, laughing.

He and Jill slunked off into the distance.

"What did he mean about seeing the both of us on the rebound?" asked Addy.

"Oh, he's ... he'll be at the country club event, also," answered Roland.

"*What* event?" Addy asked.

"Just ... a tiny get-together for some of the younger clubbers," said Roland. "Addy, I'd really love it if you could join me."

"Well ..."

"Please, Addy. *Look*! I'm as harmless as a farm mouse at a forest orgy!"

Addy glanced down at Roland's khakis. No strange and jerky movements inside his pockets this time. Maybe he *had* changed.

This was a very good sign.

Addy looked up at a fresh cloud floating above, imagining what object *this* cloud most closely resembled, finally deciding on Henry Fonda's neck wattle in *On Golden Pond.*

"Okay," exclaimed Addy, with a quiver in her voice. "Yes, I *will* go with you!"

It wasn't the prom, true, but it was still so *totally* exciting! Addy wondered if there might even be klieg lights and a deep-plush red carpet!

"Wonderful," said Roland. "And will you promise that you'll wear just what you're wearing now? I *adore* it!"

"Oh yes!" responded Addy, twirling her newly

permed hair. The curls were so tight, they were danger-ous to the touch.

Roland slipped effortlessly into his Karmann Ghia.

"In the meantime, perhaps you might like to share a shake with me over at the Cherry Pit?"

"Now?" asked Addy.

The Cherry Pit!

"Yes, now," laughed Roland.

Addy had never before been inside the Cherry Pit Diner. She only knew that a hamburger cost a rumored eight dollars and that they were alleged to serve French "crepes." Supposedly they were like pancakes but tasted more worldly.

"I would, yes," she replied. "Very much so. Let's do it!"

"Then hop yourself in," Roland said, with a head motion, turning on his cassette player, complete with the latest in "Auto Reverse & Forward" technology. "Huey Lewis," he announced. "Ain't *nothing* better! The beatin' and pleatin' heart of rock and roll!"

Addy casually hopped into the car—something she had never before attempted—but didn't bother to put on her seatbelt. She didn't want to look like an idiot.

And off they squealed.

CHAPTER FOURTEEN

Inside the "Pit"

"We'll have two more chocolate milkshakes," said Roland confidently, to the diner waitress. "And make 'em *super* thick."

Where did such confidence come from?

Addy wished she had a lot more of it. Also, money. Her father did okay, but not "IBM executive" okay.

"What do you want to achieve?" Roland asked nonchalantly, plucking a fry off his plate and popping it into his supple mouth. "What would you say your *goal* is?"

Addy barely had to think about this. She had practiced this answer in her head so many, many times.

"I want to *create*. I want to make a *difference*. I want to design art objects that have never before *existed*. Does that make sense?"

"It does," said Roland, now dipping his straw into the fresh shake that had just arrived. "I really *admire* that."

"What do *you* want?" asked Addy, also now dipping her straw into her chocolate shake. "You know, to accomplish?"

"Well, I used to think I only wanted money," answered Roland. "But I don't think I just want that anymore. I have that already. I'm looking for ... love I guess. *True* love. With someone who's not like the rest."

Addy blushed. She took another sip from her shake. She could only think, *Please don't hurt me. Whatever you do, please don't emotionally hurt me.*

"Addy," continued Roland. "I have something to say and I want you to listen closely."

"Okay," said Addy, not knowing where this was headed.

Roland took a deep breath. And began: "The famous fruit of Kashmir is picked just once a year in a remote region above the Ishtar valley. These fruits are beautiful and rare. With the exception of a specialty store in New York catering to homosexuals, these fruits are nearly impossible to find, virtually unobtainable. They are coveted by the richest of the rich. But once consumed, they are never, *ever* forgotten. Some people are allergic, but most aren't. If you're allergic, you die. Otherwise, you only crave more. *You are that fruit, Addy.*"

Was it true? Not true? Did he just make it up? Steal it from an episode of *Kung Fu*?

Addy was confused as to what the hell he was talking about but she wasn't about to start with the questions.

"I want to know so much *more* about you, Addy," Roland continued. "I want to take your thoughts, your hopes, your dreams, and pluck them from your mind and throw them high into the air. Let's together discover the beautiful constellations formed!"

"Okay," said Addy, not knowing much about astrology.

"What I'm saying is ... I'd like to invite you to the prom."

"You *what*?" Addy asked stupefied, a mouthful of shake plopping from out of her mouth and on to the plastic diner table, forming its own not-so-beautiful constellation.

"*Invite you to prom*," he slowly repeated. "Would you ever consider going with me? Would you be my girl?"

The scene was almost something out of a movie written by a man who had no idea—and never did—that teens never talked like this.

"There are no ... there no Richie girls you'd rather take?" asked Addy.

Please say no. Please say no. Please say—

"No," said Roland. "I want to take *you*."

Roland reached across the table and took Addy's hand in his. She noticed that his fingers were slender, like E.T.'s. The fingernails were manicured. Addy imagined that the whirls and swoops of his fingerprints resembled the background of a Van Gogh painting but with no screaming, open-mouthed freak.

"Yes," said Addy. "Most *definitely*."

"But let's not get ahead of ourselves," Roland said, grinning. "First there's this date at the country club. Let's consider this a—*whatya say?*—practice run of sorts?"

Addy smiled. It was *happening*. This was *unquestionably* happening!

Over the course of the next three hours, still holding hands, the two talked about so many fascinating things:

Roland's car.

Roland's car stereo system.

Roland's motorboat berthed within a private pier on Lake Erie.

Roland's cedar wardrobe to keep away any and all moths from his silk cravats.

Roland's growing anger that Huey Lewis was not allowed to sing on the recent smash hit "Do They Know It's Christmas (Even Though They're Muslim)?"

And then they proceeded to talk about Addy.

Specifically:

About how Addy would no doubt fall in love with Roland's Atomic Vantage skis.

About how Addy should really get to know Whinny better, to see that she wasn't as aloof as she first appeared, that she really was down to Earth, even though Roland had just spent a fortune on the gold-plated mini-saddle she had kept insisting on.

"So what does your father do for a living?" Roland finally asked, after showing Addy some Polaroids of his Yamaha three-wheel all-terrain vehicle that he'd used just once, driving to the movie theater to see *Escape from New York* while it was sleeting.

When Addy told him about her father, and what he did for a living and what he had accomplished, Roland laughed heartily.

"That's funny!" he said, thinking it all a joke. "You're a *funny* girl."

I'm so glad you think that's funny, Addy thought.

But she was too exhausted with joy to dare correct him.

Those eyes. Those sturdy brows.

This boy was definitely on his "brow game" today!

She wanted to hug his heart and then lick it.

To the waitress, Roland said: "Two more chocolate

shakes please!"

Could this afternoon get any better? Addy thought.

And it was at this very moment that things took a turn for the worse ... so much worse ...

Suddenly, and without warning, Pribbenow sauntered over and sat down next to Addy. He was now wearing a different silk kimono, this time with a dragon on the back eating the latest Japanese food craze called "sushi." Addy had heard about it on the national news. The dragon was using two lightning bolts as chopsticks.

Couldn't Pribbenow leave well enough alone?

To the waitress, Pribbenow said: "Actually, make that second shake for me. *She* probably shouldn't." He laughed. "I mean, you should have as many as you want, Addy. *If* you want. Whatever you're comfortable with body wise. I don't care. I like your body. It's *natural*."

"C'mon, Pribbenow," said Roland. "Lay off."

"Since when is natural bad? You'd prefer *unnatural*? Relax. Just having a snicky-snack as I wait for Jill to finish her breakdancing lessons at the mall," said Pribbenow, plucking a single fry off Addy's plate and sucking it down like a baby bird feasting on a deep-fried worm. "So! What's the words, turds?"

Roland and Addy said nothing. Pribbenow grimaced. "Ah. And so it looks like I'm not wanted here. That's cool. You can have my shake, Addy. Roland will take care of the bill."

Pribbenow smiled, winked at Roland, and nodded to the waitress.

"See you at the CC," said Pribbenow, standing.

"CC?" asked Addy.

"Country club," declared Pribbenow, blowing on his fingernails. He was wearing expensive videogame leather gloves with no tips. "The club in the country. Oh, it'll be most fun!"

Cinching his kimono tight, he gave Addy a "gun shot" with his thumb and forefinger and then slithered from out of the diner and into the parking lot, where his car—a brand new Porsche 944 in Miami Vice pelican pink—was parked horizontally across three spaces.

"I'm so sorry," said Roland as Pribbenow pulled out with a sharp squeal and a loud beep of his horn which played the opening notes to Styx's "Mr. Roboto."

"You didn't need to hear that. Sometimes I think he likes you. But that's crazy, right? Maybe not so crazy. You're pretty awesome. He's really not a bad guy. And I've known him, like, forever."

It was true.

Roland and Pribbs had attended the same elite Water-Skiing Academy in the late 70s.

Going back even further, Roland and Pribbs had shared the same governess for exactly one day before she went mad and returned to her native, war-torn El Salvador, where it was considerably safer.

Pribbenow had always been the savvy one; Roland, the sweet, perhaps not so sharp one.

Together, they made a "righteous" team.

To prove as much, just last week they had re-enacted the entire Duran Duran "Rio" video on Pribbenow's father's sailboat.

"But can we get back to talking about *you*?" said Roland. And he seemingly meant it.

152

Later, hours later, after Roland had talked about so many fascinating subjects, including stories about his Sony radio-slash-CD bathroom player, his bank account on St. Kitt's, his personal urinal splatter-guard (Ralph Lauren, Polo) he carried with him at all times (including now), he dropped Addy off a mile from her house in his Karmann Ghia, planted a huge kiss straight on to her anxiously recipient lips and waved a reverse goodbye.

Back in her room, Addy placed her bouquet of 7-Eleven carnations into a vase that was shaped like a giant ballet shoe and pressed the PLAY button on her modern telephone answering machine that was showing an astonishing **31** messages. She didn't remember the last time she had received so many. Her heart beat fast.

The new outgoing message was in her voice—as a *robot*. And it was hilarious: "Hello. I. Am. A. Robot. My. Human. Master. Is. Busy. Doing. Human. Things. Please. Leave. A. Beep. After. The. *Massage* ..."

Perhaps word had gotten around school about this amazing message and people were calling en masse.

Addy lay back on her ancient Strawberry Short-cake-themed bedsheets and wondered if it was Roland who had left all these messages, perhaps from a phone inside his car, which was all but impossible, but still ...

"Hi, it's Grimer."

Addy sighed. She didn't need this now. Not at all.

Grimer went on: *"It's 9:35. Give me a ring. That's a funny outgoing message! Why did you get rid of the rap? Okay, call back please. BEEP. Hi, it's Grimer again. 9:47. Give me a ring-a-ding ... please? BEEP. Hi, Grimer Grimer Grimer Grimer Grimer Grimer*

*here! 9:56. BEEP. Last time I'm calling tonight! Guess
who? It's 10:01 already. BEEP. I just lied. That wasn't
the last time. Where are you? I hope you're okay. 11:14.
BEEP Right about now I'm going to play 'Mary Had
a Little Lamb' on the buttons here. Two two two, three
nine nine. Two two two, three nine nine ....*

There were thirty additional messages from Grimer
but Addy would listen to them all tomorrow. Or not.

What could he possibly want to tell her?

She'd find out later. What was the rush?

There was none.

Addy felt she wouldn't be able to sleep. There was
only one thing to do. She carefully placed an LP on her
turntable and retreated back to her bed.

It was time to listen to one of her all-time favorite
alterna songs.

She planned on listening to it all night long.

It was called "Love Ain't Binary Code" and it was
almost as if it was written especially for her:

> *Love. is. not. a. binary. code.*
> *Us. Machines. have. no. feeling.*
> *Our. wires. run. cold.*
>
> *Dot matrix printers,*
> *floppydisks.*
>
> *Cathode ray monitors*
> *cannot feel this bliss!*
> *Love. is. not. a. binary. code.*
> *Us. Machines. have. no. feeling.*

Our. wires. run. cold.

When it's Ones and Zeroes,
That all computes.
But two for tea and tea for who?

It's time to re-boot!
Love. is. not. a. binary. code.
Us. Machines. have. no. feeling.
Our. wires. run. cold.

ASCII any keyboard.
The answer's always the same.
Us Personal Computers will never ever change!

CHAPTER FIFTEEN

Scouting

Addy knew the Back World well enough by this point to travel from one end of the school to the other without Grimer. She was spending most of her days back here, sometimes disappearing for hours at a time.

Her grades were suffering but it was never going to be academics that would eventually bring her fame and fortune, but rather found knick-knacks reconstituted into useless art objects.

Besides, with Grimer's help, Addy had learned how to hack into the school's computer system to access the grading logs and tests. This would take place after school was finished, in the late afternoon. During the day, Addy would either relax in the lair or just spy on those who interested her.

From above, she would listen in on the conversations happening in the teacher's lounge. There was so much gossip! Yesterday, she heard the following exchange taking place between two English teachers, Mr. Grant and Mr. Horst:

"I have to go relieve the babysitter."

"I didn't know you had kids!"

"I *don't!*"

Both of the teachers had laughed heartily. Addy was

still trying to figure it all out.

Was it some type of teacher's code?

She'd have to ask Kristina about it later.

Another morning, Addy overheard her home-ec teacher, Miss Rabensky (aka Miss Rabid), complaining to another teacher about the price of Hamburger Helper. But the conversation soon switched over to how Addy never showed up for class anymore. Miss Rabid had asked some of the other teachers if Addy skipped *their* classes also. Then she announced, "If I just had one student—one *single* student—who came in with their own recipe, who just showed the slightest bit of initiative, I would love that. That's an A for sure. Just *one* student! To cook at home. To create their own dishes. Wouldn't that be *lovely*?!"

At the next class, Addy showed up with one of her mother's handwritten recipes, one that her mother never in a million years would ever notice had gone missing:

Lemon chicken. Grated orange zest. Covered in wine spritzer. Lit afire in a make-do wok. Burned to a scarred, horrid mess. Ignored.

It was absolute garbage and Addy hated it.

Miss Rabid *also* hated it but, god, how she loved the initiative and inventiveness!

Addy received a B minus but that was okay. She'd just change it to a B plus later. Not too high, not too low, just mediocre enough for no one of any importance to ever take notice.

Addy had quickly gotten used to her new, exciting life within the school.

So had Lucy, who was enjoying her time in the

Back World by spying on the kids from above, much like she did with her ants within their numerous farms. "It's fascinating," she told Kristina one day, while both were relaxing in the Lair, watching their daytime soaps. "All of the different cliques are no different than any subset of ants. They're separate entities but they all work together as one single organism. Witness the entire school rooting for the football team."

Kristina had nodded, attention more focused on the new and exciting relationship forming on *General Hospital* between Ned Quartermaine and a delightful 18-year-old candy striper who "dug" sex and jazzercise.

All five of the "Hang Gang" loved to eat their lunches back here in the Lair, avoiding the cafeteria altogether. But on this Thursday afternoon in April, a few days after Addy's wonderful date at the diner, with the weather outside at last turning warm and the purple forget-me-nots finally emerging from out of a sodden ground, Addy had the Lair entirely to herself. She didn't know exactly where the rest of the Hang Gang was at the moment but she assumed they were all in class. She didn't know where Grimer was at the moment, either, but didn't necessarily care. She was too busy prepping for her big country club date the following night.

What would she ever talk about?

Addy had no idea.

But she would *not* arrive unprepared.

She flipped through a copy of an exceedingly large school-library book: *Diversional Activities for Rich Assholes.*

Inside were some very interesting tidbits!

For instance, Addy had never realized that anyone making below $25,000 was not allowed to play golf until 1975.

That would make for a *great* conversation starter!

Addy had also not realized that there was never a championship downhill skier who was a Hasidic Jew.

This was *fascinating*!

By the time the final bell rang for the day, Addy had finished the book and had written down three more potential talking points for the country club get-together:

There had once been a Negro League for badminton.

The most popular name for a championship racing yacht was "Dirty Little Oars."

Nobody ever failed to look like a fucking idiot playing lawn croquet.

Addy was ready!

As she applied a dab of lipstick with her cleavage (it really was the *only* accurate way to do it), Addy heard the sound of footsteps in the passageway, quickly approaching the Lair ...

Please don't be the janitor, thought Addy. *How to explain away this one?*

Grimer walked in.

He didn't appear at all surprised by Addy's method for applying lipstick and yet he did look grim.

"What's the matter?" Addy asked, not bringing up the fact that Grimer was wearing a top hat without a top. "Were you drunk when you kept calling the other night? You called a *million* times."

"*Addy*," Grimer said. "I have something to tell you. I've been endlessly debating whether I should even do this. And it may not be easy for me to say."

"Because of your weakness caused by a lack of Vitamin C?" asked Addy.

"No," said Grimer.

"You take a crap in the principal's chair again?"

"Not today," said Grimer. "It's far worse. A few days ago, when I was traveling above the C Hallway, just minding my own business, I overheard that horrible Pubenow talking to his new girlfriend."

"*Pribb*enow," Addy corrected.

"Still minding my own business, I eavesdropped. They were talking about what's going to happen at the country club tomorrow. I don't think you should go, Addy."

"What did they say?"

"I couldn't make all of it out, as I was minding my own business just above the hallway listening, but I *really do not* think you should go."

"You're jealous," said Addy, with perhaps a little too much conviction. "That's all it is! You don't want me to be happy! You don't want me to date Roland because *you'd* rather be with me!"

Grimer looked as if he was about to cry. It wasn't a good look. In fact, it was horrifying.

"I'm telling you that you shouldn't go, Addy. Whether you do or not is up to you. I can't do more than that. I honestly can't."

"He asked me to the prom," said Addy.

"I know. Lucy told me. Yes, I'm jealous. I admit that. But I am only telling you this as a friend: *do not go tomorrow night*. Please."

"Fine," said Addy petulantly.

"Fine," said Grimer, heading over to his art studio area. He stared at Addy a moment. It was unclear what exactly that last "fine" meant exactly. *Would she go? Not go?* Either way, he'd done his job. He had tried. He pulled out a huge piece of canvas and started to furiously paint.

It was a grand painting and Grimer had been working on it for days now.

Addy left the Lair before she could see what this new painting was.

She could only imagine.

The last painting had been yet another nude of Mrs. Wilkins, the sixty-five-year-old gym teacher, this one featuring a whistle hanging around her neck and landing softly where it never should have landed.

Addy prayed she'd never have to see anything like it ever again.

CHAPTER SIXTEEN

Will They Ever Get It?!

Saturday morning. Yet another awful breakfast to plan with the atrocious Riccardacchios!

Addy's sister was elaborately choosing *just* the perfect outfit. On the wall next to her, on a shelf, was a neat line of aerosol deodorants, in alphabetical order: Cinnamon Bun Tickle to Wild Cherry Soft & Dri, her personal favorite, the one she always wore to her job as a greeter at a fondue restaurant inside the Air Florida terminal at O'Hare.

Addy was sitting on her sister's large bed, spread clean with a Navajo white cotton bedspread.

The two sisters hadn't spoken in weeks, and—although they tended only to get along in the best of circumstances (say, when joyfully watching their mother perform Jane Fonda aerobics in layered-slouch socks on a slippery wood floor while drunk)—the princess did occasionally provide solid advice, especially when it came to dating.

"Is he gorgeous?" Mary Anne asked. "This boy you like?"

"*Beyond* gorge," said Addy, slipping seamlessly into Ramba talk.

"And what about that shit-smelling weirdo in the

Thriller outfits? What's his name? Gumby?"

"Grimer," corrected Addy.

"Him," said Mary Anne. "Doesn't he like you also?"

"He does," said Addy. "But ... well, he's *different*."

"I thought you liked *different*," Mary Anne said. She enunciated "different" to the point where it really sounded *different*, or at least different enough when coming from someone who wasn't truly and sincerely different.

"I do but ... I don't know," said Addy. "I'm just so *confused*!"

"Why?" said Mary Anne. "The hotty already invited you to the prom! *You won*! What are you worried about?!"

"He did but there's something very vulnerable about Grimer," said Addy, failing to mention that Grimer's vulnerability came directly from raising himself as an orphan inside a public school and primarily subsisting on stolen tater tots that inevitably led to a Vitamin C deficiency.

"When you were in high school," Addy asked, "did you know anyone who wasn't invited to prom?"

Mary Anne laughed. "My friend never got invited. You remember Robyn? Real Yoid? Studied all the time? She's now pre-med at Northwestern. Poor thing."

"And you're now working as greeter at the Fonduely Yours restaurant," said Addy.

"Yes," her sister said proudly. "I have been blessed."

She atomized herself with a spritz of Enjoli, the eight hour perfume for the twenty-four hour woman.

"I like that outfit," declared Addy, changing the

subject and pointing. "I'd wear *that* one."

"You think so?" asked Mary Anne, posing before her mirror. "You don't think that the tube top sequin clashes with the fuchsia and turquoise moon boots?"

"No, it's good, *real* good."

"You know, Addy. I'd stop feeling sorry for yourself if I were you. It doesn't make you look any more attractive."

"Gee, thanks."

"Okay, clear out," said the princess. "I have to concentrate on faking my laugh."

Addy got down from the bed and walked out of the room. Her sister launched into a fake laugh. To Addy, it sounded like the final scene from *Amadeus*, the one that takes place inside an 19th century madhouse.

But it was effective. Maybe that was the key to a happy life: *learning how to successfully fake your laugh.*

Out in the hallway, Addy ran straight into smiling Justin. *Of course!*

"How's the Richie thing going, *retardo*?!"

"Not bad," said Addy, earnestly. "I have a date with the boy I'm going to prom with on Saturday at the Restricted Pines country club!"

In a typical encounter, the following would then occur: Addy would ask Justin if he had any boogers to pick somewhere and *shouldn't he get moving*?, and Justin would respond that *the boogers were right here* in his nose and that *maybe she should be eating them?* and she'd reply, "Gross" and then he would say, "Get broke!"

"You okay?" Justin asked, instead. He seemed a tad

disappointed that the typical scenario wasn't playing out.

"Justin," asked Addy. "Does it not bother you that you're a Yoid and always will be? You have no aspirations to become a Richie? Or to ever hang out with one?"

"No," said Justin, confused by the question, smiling. "I'm kind of happy with who I am, Addy."

"I wish I could be, too," Addy said.

"So what's stopping you?" Justin asked.

Addy sighed. Her brother wouldn't understand until next year, when the high school's social scene became that much more intense and when it all began to "count." But she appreciated her little brother's immature, silly advice, as ignorant and naïve as it was.

"I don't know, Justin. But thank you. You're sweet."

Her brother wasn't so bad after all!

For old time's sake, Addy said, "Don't you have boogers to pick somewhere?"

Justin grinned. He was on to Addy's game. "Right here in my nose. Eat 'em, sis!"

Addy walked past the guest room where the Chonger was staying. She took a peek inside. He was wearing black denim pants with a red handkerchief tied around each ankle, and a green leather coat, unbottoned. He was practicing dance moves while blasting B96, Chicago's best radio for the hottest in Top Forty. An advertisement was playing. Chonger was mouthing along to it:

"How to BreakDance Like U Mean It! Everybody wants to but not every one can! Now even YOU can, in the comfort of your own living room! Head Spins! The Shakes! Wobbles! Jack Hammers! Head Slides! The Pelvic Slithers! 'Buddha' Twizzles! Up Rocking! Floor

Rocking! The Spider! The Egyptian! The Arm Wave! You've seen and watched in wonder as professional dancers have spun their urban way right into your suburban heart. Now you too can dance just like those who live in the cities! 45 minutes taught to you by the lead star of Slippin' into Dat Groove Stream, *Renoldo 'Slappy-Pang' Martinez! 45 minutes of head-spinning, magical dancing wonder! On VHS and Beta! Only $79.99! Put Your Best Foot Forward! And then Back! Now spin! It is remarkable!"*

"C'mon, let's *go* already," interrupted her father, pushing Addy aside. He was buttoning up his dress shirt and wending his way—always *wending*—through the typical familial chaos. Addy wondered if her father would ever be capable of buttoning up his dress shirt if he wasn't on the move.

"The Rettardios are arriving any minute!" he barked, rushing into his bedroom, and then over to the closet, ripping off his shirt, choosing another exactly like it.

Addy followed.

"How's the prom thing going?" he asked semi-concerned.

"Good, daddy," responded Addy, sitting down on the bed. "*Really* good! I was asked to prom!"

Her father sighed and stopped fidgeting with his shirt's incredibly complicated buttons. He'd take care of that impossibility later. For now, it was time to talk with his pleasantly non-threatening middle child who was forever and always perplexed about one tiny useless drama or another.

Sitting down on the edge of his own bed, he patted

the spot beside him, just next to where Addy was already sitting.

"Talk to your ol' man. What's the matter? You're crying. And you're holding one shoe that doesn't belong to you. Is everything okay?"

"You said that last time, daddy! And I'm not crying. I just told you I was asked to prom!"

"I loathe life, honey. I'm *very* tired."

"You're *always* saying that!" cried Addy. "You're impossible!"

"I never did reach cruising altitude," her father mumbled. "Just ... too much *turbulence*."

Her father was unbearable!

"You know," her father continued unabated, "I always did want to become a famous writer. And publish that novel about the midget who lives on the shoulders of a shipwrecked World War II soldier on a Pacific island, but ..."

Addy rolled her eyes. *This story again....*

"Honey, come back!" he cried suddenly.

He was talking to Addy, who hadn't yet left.

Addy stood and left. She didn't want to be anywhere in the vicinity of the poor man when he attempted to knot his bow-tie. That was going to be all sorts of *ugly*.

Addy made her way down the hallway and back into Mary Anne's room. She didn't know where else to head.

Now, instead of her laugh, the Princess was faking her *smile*.

"Ethnics like to smile a lot," she said to Addy, by way of explanation. "I've had a *lot* of guys, Addy. But this one, he's gone absolutely nutso for me. Even after *two* weeks. I know our family would be a lot happier if I married someone who lived on our side of the lake. And that I'm marrying down. But love is a funny thing."

She burst out laughing. Addy was pretty sure this laugh was real, and yet it still sounded unhinged.

"Okay leave," she said, pushing Addy out. "I now have to match my hand movements to what I'm saying. This is what ethnics do."

Addy walked out of the room and down the stairs to the kitchen to find her mother sipping from her favorite WINE IS FINE plastic cup and removing pimentos from green olives. She was replacing them with Reese's Pieces, the same candy the space monkey who fell from the sky and caused havoc liked to snack on so much when he wasn't causing havoc.

"Mom, can I ask you a question?"

"As long as it's not about these olives," replied her mother.

"When did you first know you were in love with daddy?"

"Oh, that's *eathee*," she replied, slurring the word so that "easy" sounded like "ether," one of her all-time favorite anesthetics. "When he impregnated me on a nighttime empty L train while synth music blasted. C'mon. Help me. The Refractios will be here any minute. They are *impossible* to please."

She clapped her hands twice. This could only be the signal for Chonger to approach.

It was.

Chonger approached.

With *vigor*.

"Chonger Crumbles!" he loudly announced, still dancing, handing a paper bag to Addy's mother.

Addy's mom accepted the bag and dumped the contents down onto the kitchen counter—a mound of cookie crumbles.

"Chonger Crumbles? What is *that*?"

"The next food craze," announced her mother, oblivious to Chonger's silent prancing. "Chonger invented it. I really think they're gonna be a smash!"

"I thought you wanted to be the next Famous Anus," Addy asked. "Selling gigantic cookies? Wasn't that your dream?"

"People are getting lazier," her mother announced, confidently. "The late '80s will all be about pre-packaged convenience! We're crumbling the cookies *for* people."

It was good to see the gleam back in her mother's glazed eyes. And at least this idea was original, unlike her past ideas, such as the KALVON KLAYN bootleg jeans or the Smurfs knockoffs, Tiny Lil' Muffs.

These weren't great ideas, or even legal, but Addy still hoped that her mother would one day find success. If only to get her mother out of the goddamn house for a few hours each day like the rest of her friends' mothers, including Lucy's mom, who was now working part-time as a greeter at the Spaghetti Factory. She wore a Styrofoam derby hat.

The "bad nerve" storms her mother suffered from for years were only getting worse. Addy prayed she wouldn't ever again have to witness her mother in a straightjacket with huge shoulder pads.

169

It was a modern look but not an overly attractive one.

"I think it's time that we had a talk," said her mother suddenly, to her own shadow against the wall.

"Okay," said Addy.

Chonger went prancing off.

Typically when her mother started conversing with the Shadow People, it was meant for Addy.

Both Addy and her mother made their way into the living room and over to the "just rappin' couch." Her mother sat down on one end. "When was the last time we did this? You know, just talked, girl to girl?" she asked.

Addy thought for a moment. "When you taught me all about sex by giving me your copy of *Peyton Place*?"

"God, I so loved that book!" said her mother, dreamily.

"You really did," said Addy.

"But first grade was just too young. I *know* that now. I apologize. Which is why I want you to have *this*."

She handed over a well-worn copy of *Our Bodies, Ourselves*. "I underlined the most important parts and I double-circled the words that mean the most to me: 'solo' and 'self-experimentation.' *Oh, Addy, baby!* You're growing up so fast! Before you know it, you'll be heading south of the lake and meeting your own ethnic! Are you happy?"

"I think so," said Addy.

"Go, honey," said her mother. "You won't regret it. Maybe you will. I don't know."

Addy didn't know what her mother was referring to—*perhaps prom, maybe not*—but that was okay.

"Wait! Your father tells me we forgot the anniversary of your first period?" her mother blurted. "That happened?"

"Yes," said Addy.

"I'm so sorry, honey. I wasn't even aware that you experienced your first period, let alone the anniversary."

Addy sighed. "You weren't? You were telling me what was happening from behind the bathroom door."

"Oh, *that*? I thought I was teaching you how to knit."

Addy liked her freedom just as much as any teenager but she was beginning to think there was such a thing as maybe *too much freedom*.

If she ever did become a parent herself, Addy thought, she would never let her kids get away with anything. She'd be on top of them all the time! They would appreciate that! And they would be all the better off for it!

"Go get me a cranberry juice," her mother announced to the wall. "And make it *sing*, baby."

It was a good talk.

The doorbell rang. A leaf blower at full throttle on a Sunday morning. The suburban mating call.

"They're here," Addy's mother announced sadly. "No doubt with their freshly baked crescents and steaming hot coffee already deliciously prepared. These people are *revolting*!"

Addy's mother walked into the kitchen, scooping up a large mound of crumbs and dumping them onto a paper towel. She balled the towel into a wet, leaking fist, making her way over to the front door.

Addy sighed.

She didn't need any of this nonsense, not in the least.

She headed straight up to her pink-encrusted sanctuary. She had more *important* things to think about.

Such as picking out her wardrobe for tonight's CC event!

But first, she'd slow-dance with Yarnkin to one of her favorite new alternative songs, "Love is More Than Styrofoam."

The lyrics rang out so loud, so true, almost as if they had been written especially for Addy's very special relationship with her six-foot tall Frankenstein-type monster who scared the hell out of just about everyone else in the neighborhood:

Weren't my first choice for a lover,
Or my second or even third.
But I have no room for complainin'
you're no less exotic than a stuffed bird.

Yearning for Yarnkin,
Yearning for Yarnkin.

Remember when I had no friends,
We stayed up and you did my hair?
We broke into the town pool,
Skinny dipping in our underwear?

I'm gonna find a new honey,
Who looks just like you.
But the difference might be the flesh and the blood,
And your strong, toxic smell of glue.

I let myself get tangled
In your luke-warm embrace
But now I must move on ...

Yarnkin, Yarnkin, how I wish you were real!
To kiss you in the hallways, to let you cop a feel!
To share milkshakes, to write poetry,
But for now I have to say goodbye,
For the real world beckons,
I'll save you a steaming slice of love pie.

CHAPTER SEVENTEEN

Party Time!

"I've driven past so many times," her father had said as he dropped Addy off a hundred yards beyond the entrance to the country club.

The club's name, RESTRICTED PINES was spelled out in topiary, trimmed to perfection by a hardworking non-member. "But I've never been inside. Are you sure I can't drive through the front gates to just ... look around?"

Addy had shaken her head. *Not a chance. See ya!* She would call for him to pick her up whenever she was ready. Or, better yet, Roland could just drive her straight home and drop her off a quarter mile past her driveway.

Her father had blown her a kiss.

Whatever.

He drove off in his "Tweedledumb."

Fuchsia round-paper lanterns hung from trees that lined the long S-shaped drive that led to the clubhouse. Even the geese seemed smugly pleased to be here. Addy wondered if they, too, were genealogically screened for racial and religious impurities before being allowed on to the property.

The clubhouse loomed just ahead. Fancy young country-clubbers in their upmarket dress and fluorescent neon cummerbunds milled about before the solid oak doors without a care in the world.

Addy confidently made her way through. Her petite canary-yellow cocktail dress from the subjugation mall kiosk, with a frilly baby blue headband and a large pink bow, three feet wide by three feet long, was causing fellow partiers to nod approvingly as she passed.

She's one of us.

She belongs here.

Where had this mystery girl come from? She was simply dramatic*!*

Walking into the clubhouse foyer, Addy saw Roland standing alone next to a rented food fountain overflowing with liquid chocolate.

White chocolate.

He was grinning widely.

This was almost *too* easy.

"Hello," Roland said, as Addy approached.

"Hello," replied Addy.

No more "hi" for her!

So far, so clutch!

"You look fantastic," said Roland. "Really ... *really* super excellent!"

Roland's brain was clearly working overtime. Addy found it *orbs*, which meant "adorbs."

"Thank you," Addy replied, straightening and toying with her gigantic pink bow. It was exceedingly heavy and hurting her neck, which drooped forward toward her toes. *But god, it looked good!* "I was hoping you'd like what I wore."

"Well, I do," said Roland. "I'm really happy you're

here tonight. I've been thinking about you non-stop."

Addy thought: *That is so, so, so, so sweet!*

How should she put this without sounding desperate?

"That is so, so, so, so sweet," she said.

She was too excited to even rewrite the thought in her own head and then say it differently.

Addy looked over Roland's outfit. She noticed he was wearing his typical awesome Richie ensemble, complete with knit necktie, and yet his shoes appeared to be more vibrant than was typically the case. Instead of smoky topaz brown butter-soft Gucci loafers without socks, Roland was wearing orange tasseled loafers with bright green laces and white socks.

Even for Addy—who greatly appreciated *different* as much as or *more* than anyone else—this was a bit unsettling.

Roland's eyes caught Addy's glance. He blushed.

Perhaps he was trying—in his own strange and bizarre manner—to fit in more with Addy's world just as she was trying so hard to fit into his?

If it wasn't so painful to look at it would have almost been semi-delightful.

An elegant black man wearing fancy whites approached holding a silver platter. On it were the tiniest yellow foodies Addy had ever seen, smaller than even her mother's drunk gigantic cookie mistakes.

"Quiche," announced Roland proudly, grabbing one with a cloth napkin. "I *adore* quiche!"

Addy saw the black server roll his eyes.

Probably just jealous.

Addy accepted a napkin and grabbed a few of these

incredibly strange edible delights off the tray. They were as dense as a "black hole," and probably just as mysterious. She coquettishly nibbled one.

Eggy.

They reminded Addy of her mother's "Overmicrowaved Egg Until It Tasted Like Kitchen Sponge" dish.

"Good, huh?" Roland asked. "C'mon, I want to introduce you to a few of my friends."

"Oh no!" exclaimed Addy. "Come on, Roland! Last time didn't go so well, right?"

Roland smiled. "I have a strong feeling it'll be *better* this go round."

Young Richies milled exotically in the foyer, slowly making their opulent way into a larger room with a stage in the back.

Addy and Roland followed the group in.

The miniature horse Whinny, thankfully, was nowhere to be seen. Addy assumed the country club did not allow miniature horses to become members, which was just fine with her. There was most likely a country club deeper into the suburbs that did.

"These are my country club friends," announced Roland, gesturing. "This is Ruffle, Gleam, Yale, Chlamydia, and Chaffon."

"Hi!" said Addy, upbeat. "Yachting is one of the most popular and enjoyable past times available to the water loving sportsman!"

Ruffle looked over to Gleam, who nodded. *All right, then! This girl is okay!*

"Well, we'll see you after the show," exclaimed Roland to his friends, leading Addy to the side of the room.

"They were absolutely *loving* what I was saying!" said Addy.

She herself couldn't quite believe it.

"They certainly were," said Roland, impressed not only with Addy's incredible knowledge but also with the fact that he, too, knew this particular bit of yachting trivia. *They had a lot more in common than he initially thought!*

"Addy!" screamed a short brunette in a sequined lace taffeta gown.

"Jill," said Addy, carefully, defensively.

It was Jill Standish, currently the school's "number one," and Pribbenow's latest girlfriend.

"Addy, I wanted to tell you that I'm so glad you're here. I think you have a lot to offer. *Mucho* apologies!"

"Apology accepted," responded Addy, not realizing until now that Jill was multilingual.

"I want to introduce you to my date tonight," said Jill. "You might know him from one of your classes. Jeremy Beldam."

Addy did indeed recognize Jeremy. He was known as Someone Who Was Once Caught Holding Hands with His Grandmother at the Mall, at least according to the digital board in Dr. Mulligan's office. The lowest of the low.

"You and Pribbenow are no longer dating?" Addy asked.

Jill said nothing, merely left.

"Babe!" announced Pribbenow, approaching.

Here we go, thought Addy.

"Babe!" Pribbenow again said.

Roland still didn't respond.

"Babe!" Pribbenow yelled a third time, even louder.

Wait. Was he talking to her and not to Roland?

"Are you talking to *me*?" Addy asked, finally.

"Who else?" asked Pribbenow. "I'm so glad you could make it!"

Addy was stunned. Louder than intended, she announced, "What about all of those rude things you said to me a few days ago? In the parking lot? And then at the diner?"

"*That*?" asked Pribbenow. "Ha! Come on now. That was just for grins, baby! Some jicky-jock to pass the sludge of timmy-time!"

"A jicky-jock?" asked Addy. "You mean a *joke*? I don't believe you."

"We've had our differences, yes," said Pribbenow. "But I am so happy to see you here! I hope you have a grand ol' time tonight! No chocolate milkshakes, I'm afraid! But have as much food as you want! Or whatever you're comfortable with!" And then to Roland, Pribbenow slithered, "I will catch *you* on the rebound. I have to go find my date."

"Why aren't you and Jill going out any more?" asked Addy, genuinely curious.

Pribbenow scuttled away. Addy noticed that he, too, was wearing a pair of ugly tasseled-loafers, bright red with banana-yellow laces.

The room lights went off and back on.

"They're signaling for the show to start," said Roland excitedly, moving closer to the stage. He approached but didn't stop. He was now climbing up *onto* the stage. And sticking out a hand to help Addy up.

Addy wasn't the only one being helped on to the stage. Other country club Richies and their dates were also climbing up, both to Addy's left and right.

Pribbenow was helping up *his* date, a girl Addy didn't know at all but someone she could tell was way beyond her comfort zone. Addy felt sorry for her. *She used to be one of them. And not that long ago, too!*

The room lights blinked on and off one more time, and then off for good.

From the stage, Addy squinted through the overhead spotlights, trying to make out just who exactly was in the audience, but couldn't see a thing. She sensed, however, that the room was filling quickly.

"What's going on?" Addy whispered to Roland. "Why are we on stage?"

"It's a contest," said Pribbenow. "Ugliest shoes. Just watch. You don't have to do a thing. It'll be fun!"

So that's why all the country clubbers were wearing ugly shoes!

A grown man wearing a safari explorer's hat leaped on to the stage. Addy recognized him as being Captain Late Night, host of the reruns and old movies on the local Chicago channel 44. There was a rumor that had been going around for ages that the Cap'n was sleeping with Moona Lisa, the horror hostess who was also on channel 44.

"*Wellllllllll*," said Captain Late Night, imitating President Ronald Reagan. "Here we go. It's certainly going to be a wonderful event here tonight!"

As hard as Addy tried—and she was now trying very hard indeed—she could not in any way imagine this guy ever sleeping with Moona Lisa, or anyone else for that matter.

The Cap'n placed a hand over the head of the first Richie. The crowd applauded vigorously.

"You look *mah*-velous," said the Captain, now in the role of Billy Crystal's Fernando, the hottest character on *Saturday Night Live*. "Just *mah*-velous!"

To Addy, the wait for the Captain's arrival was unbearable, similar to those terrible few minutes waiting nude, or semi-nude, on an examination table for her doctor or psychologist to knock and enter.

When the Cap'n's hand at last reached over Roland's head, Addy could tell that the audience's reaction was louder, more sustained, almost as if they couldn't help themselves.

Animalistic.

Carnal.

Venereal.

When the applause finally died down, Captain 44 moved on down the line.

"Roland, they *love* you!" whispered Addy. "Can't you hear them applauding?"

"I think they love you, *too*!" replied Roland, and brought Addy close to him.

God, he smelled so delicious. Like a hand-cranked dittoed test run through a bulky, pungent-smelling sheen of clear solvent!

Captain 44 reached the end of the line. He adjusted his safari hat.

181

"I think we have a winner!" he announced. He looked to be in a rush, almost as if he wanted to immediately drive back to the station so that he could introduce an important rerun of *M*A*S*H*.

Addy wondered if it might just be her very favorite episode: the one in which Klinger falls in love with a North Korean chicken.

Roland reached over and grabbed Addy's hand.

Even if Roland wasn't the winner, Addy thought, *she had already won.*

This was like a dream but more intense; similar to that time Addy hallucinated she was a famous princess after consuming a horrid meal of nachos with melted, mottled yellow cheese at Wrigley Field.

"And that winner would be …"

Addy held her breath. She dare not let out even so much as a tiny gulp.

" … the man wearing the orange tasseled loafers with bright green laces! And his *lovely* date!"

It was Roland! And her!

Addy squealed.

This was too much!

Addy's heart Mary Lou Rettoned.

And *stuck* the landing.

Addy knew that she would never, *ever*—not until the day she'd eventually lose her virginity on a bed of pink plastic rose petals spread across a lumpy futon mattress in her freshman dorm at a second-tier art school while "Don't Dream It's Over" blasted on her lesbian room-mate's graffitied cassette player—be any happier than she was at this very moment.

Someone stepped forth and handed Addy a bouquet of grocery store, cut-rate, variety flowers.

The price tag had already been lovingly removed.

They had thought of everything!

"I'm so happy," whispered Roland to Addy. "I want to tell you something."

"Yes," Addy responded. She turned to face Roland. He looked more gorgeous than Corey Feldman and Corey Haim put together.

From here on out, Addy would think of him as the "third Corey."

"You look *volcanic* tonight," he said.

"Volcanic?"

"I roast for you."

"I don't get it," said Addy.

"I don't either," said Roland.

"But then why did you say it?" asked Addy.

Roland smiled. He didn't know. He didn't care. *It all didn't matter!*

Tonight was Addy's *magnum opus.*

This moment would last forever.

Addy closed her eyes, hands on her stomach, and floated deep within herself.

She wanted to *live* within this feeling.

CHAPTER EIGHTEEN

Truth Hurts, Don't It?

But her reverie did not last.

After hugging Roland, Addy headed to the country club's bathroom to clean her streaked mascara after all of her joyful crying (she hadn't cried this hard since, *when*? She forgot. Last night? A few minutes ago?) ... but stopped suddenly when she heard a loud, blaring noise.

It sounded like music.

Coming from *outside* the country club.

Were the caddies holding an unauthorized orgy?

Roland had alluded to such while munching on fries the other night at the diner. These low-lifes were allowed a very generous 15 minutes per year to unleash their most primitive and Earthly low-rent cravings.

She most definitely did *not* want to miss this!

Addy walked out of the club's front door.

She squinted and could make out a small figure standing on the 18th hole of the golf course, holding a "ghetto boom box" high above his head.

He was lit only by the full moon and a large array of high-powered halogen security lights.

No orgy taking place amongst the primitive class, sadly.

But who was this guy? And what was he doing here?

Was he trying to impress a woman?

Addy strained to hear the song that was being played. After a moment, she recognized it.

"This Jesus Must Die" from *Jesus Christ Superstar.*

Good song, Addy thought. *But a bit odd for a romantic choice, right? She herself might have chosen something by Peter Gabriel or the Smiths, but to each their own ... everyone wooed differently ...*

Addy stepped forward.

Oh my god.

"Grimer," Addy scream-whispered. "*My god.* Grimer!"

Why would security ever allow such a creature onto such a pristine property, especially after seeing that he was wearing a Pac-Man-themed bowtie with the security tag still on it, obviously stolen from the mall?

Addy quickly walked over to him.

"What are you doing here?!" she hissed.

"Addy, I love you!"

"Shhhhhh," responded Addy. "Did you hear what I asked?"

"I'm here to *save* you," answered Grimer. "I snuck in!"

"Save me from what? This couldn't *wait*?"

Addy saw Grimer's outfit. It was a gag tuxedo T-shirt with cafeteria hairnets for shoes and Bermuda shorts that ended just above the ankles.

There would be no makeover for the Grimer.

Not now, not *ever.*

Some people were just who they were and always would be—*horrendous dressers.*

"Addy," said Grimer slowly, patiently. "Do you know why Roland and you just won the contest?"

"Because he has the worst tasseled loafers," stated Addy, leaning awkwardly forward because of her large pink bow, three feet wide by three feet long. "They were uglier than the rest."

"No, Addy. They weren't voting on the ugliest loafers. They were voting on the worst date. The Yoidiest. You won. Or in this case *lost*. Hang on a second—"

Grimer tamped down his hair that was still on fire, a few smoke wisps curling their way to the full moon above.

Addy felt nauseated. Not *adorable* nauseated, but *humiliatingly* nauseated. Like that time she projectile vomited after hearing "Rapper's Delight" for the first time. Sadly, it was in her orthodontist's office.

"This is what you were trying to tell me," said Addy weakly. She could barely get the words out. "And I didn't want to listen."

Grimer held up a Xeroxed piece of yellow paper. It read:

THIS FRIDAY!
UGLY TASSELED-LOAFER PARTY!

Bring Yoidiest date! Wear ugliest shoes!
Whoever has "ugliest loafers," <u>wins!</u>
Ramba Forever!
At the Country Club

("In the Reagan Trickle Down Wing")

"I was just minding my own business while going through Pribbenow's locker and found *this*."

"Oh my god," mumbled Addy. "Oh no, no ..."

It felt as if Addy's heart Greg Lugainis'd off the diving board that was her chest.

"Once a Yoid, always a Yoid," said Grimer soothingly. "I'm so sorry, Addy. I love you so much."

"You tried to warn me, Grimer," said Addy, weakly. "You told me not to go, but I did anyway. Oh, I'm so *stupid*!"

"We need to get you home," announced Grimer, gently leading Addy over the parking lot.

"Did you steal another car?" Addy asked, barely able to get the words out.

"Better," said Grimer. "A gorgeous carriage. Pulled by a purebred Andalusian Spanish dancing horse! But no shit bag, unfortunately. I just couldn't find one big enough."

Addy didn't even want to look.

But she did anyway.

There, at the entrance, was indeed a carriage drawn by a horse.

"It's ... very nice," she responded, at last.

Addy didn't know all too much about Spanish championship purebreds but she did know a miniature horse when she saw one. It was Roland's Whinny, decked out in party velvet. Her tail was super crimped with upbangs. *Cucumber cool.* Her saddle was an oversized cable knit. *Homey chic.*

The horse was, indeed, without a shit bag.

Addy wondered if this creature was just happy to be

as far away as possible from the exhausting pressure of constantly having to live up to "Gold Ribbon miniature animal" perfection.

"Enter, m'lady," Grimer announced grandly, placing a Tyrolean Bavarian Alpine hat on top of his head.

Grimer adjusted the feather in his hat and helped Addy climb aboard the carriage, which, upon closer inspection, was nothing more than a dumpster outfitted with large rubber wheels. On second notice, the feather in Grimer's hat was nothing more than a leaf of cafeteria lettuce.

Grimer snapped the reins on Whinny's tiny back.

Slowly—more slowly than Addy had ever moved in a vehicle, even more slowly than she ever thought *capable* of moving—the jury-rigged carriage pulled out of the country's club parking lot, with an ungodly squeal.

Grimer confidently stuck out his left arm, elbow bent, palm high, signaling a right turn.

Whinny let out a high-pitched, terrified cry.

It was *super* cute.

Addy wondered if she would ever forget this night or if it would be just like any other night in which she was picked up by a stolen miniature horse and driven onto I-290 in a dumpster vehicle, awkwardly attempting to merge with any and all automobiles doing sixty-five and above.

Addy popped on her miniature cassette player "Walkman" headphones and listened to one of her favorite new *Tive Tive* songs, "Here Comes That Yummy Heartbreak."

She *needed* this now. The perfect antidote for a most

dreadful evening.

Something to make her feel even more *dreadful.*

It was almost as if these lyrics were written especially for her.

In times like these, when there was no other choice, it was best to wallow even deeper into that depressive funk:

Ooooh, here it comes,
That yummy yummy heartbreak.
It feels so good
Like straddling the bed's edge,
There's no better feeling
Give yourself a hug
You deserve it ....
Number one champion!
Here is your award!
For love!

The song was atrocious. It was no doubt sung by a group of mediocrities with winged hairdos and nylon getups who would soon be earning their livings teaching children how to play the instruments that they, themselves, could never make a career playing, but Addy turned up the song as loud as it would go, even louder than the horrified screeches coming from Whinny and the bottom of the dumpster that was now throwing sparks.

Had Roland known what the contest was all about? Or was he still standing on stage, wondering where Addy had disappeared to, looking more and more confused, replaying in his mind what exactly "You look volcanic" actually meant?

Either way, Addy didn't dare to look back.

Ooooh, here it comes ...
That yummy yummy heartbreak.
A deliciously horrible stink that smells so ungoodly bad.
The best goodly-bad stink you've ever lovedly-had.

CHAPTER NINETEEN

Shopping for the Truth

Was there any place on Earth better than the indoor shopping mall on a warm, beautiful spring afternoon? Noises, smells, temperatures all regulated just so, zero surprises, no potential for misadventure, an endless loop of mindless commercial grazing. Center planters filled with artificial trees with just the barest minimum of dirt coatings. Imitation marble benches that, even if real, would have looked gauche. Fountains clogged with videogame tokens and candy wrappers and pop-tops and the inevitable prosthetic limb.

Addy adored the mall, this neutral ground where a Yoid could hang with a Zoid who could hang with a Zat who could hang with a Zinky Znu.

A Switzerland for the high school set, with worse chocolate.

It was April, the cruelest month. Addy forgot why.

Hay fever? The start of Cubs season? That religious holiday in which Chicago Jews were forced to eat unleavened deep-dish pizza for a week?

Regardless, it was within this gloriously tiled and neoned leave-nothing-to-chance, fully-thought-out retailed reality that everything was A-minus okay. Even the kids caught shoplifting and who were now stuck in the large glass "penalty box" hanging from the third-floor ceiling by a single, fraying rope, didn't seem particularly miserable.

But within the Electric Salamander, Kristina *was* miserable—a rare mood.

"He broke up with me," she said to Addy. "He fucking *broke up* with me!"

"I'm so sorry," Addy said again, for what seemed like the hundredth time. "I can't imagine why anyone would ever want to break up with you. Especially a hydrocephalic rocker on a minor crimes against humanity charge."

"No, that was the old one," Kristina said. "I'm talking about the drummer in the all-white alternative and synth-pop band. The one who only plays standing up. The fifty-something. The one who has delusions that he's one of the members of Morris Day and the Time."

In truth, Addy knew very well why this guy—as well as all the others—had good reason to break up with Kristina, and it had a lot to do with Kristina's habit of licking and sucking vegetables in public as if they were genitals.

But who was Addy to say anything?

She had won the "Ugliest Yoid" contest last week.

To each her own.

"You have so much to offer," Addy lied to Kristina, trying to be as convincing as possible. "And is a fifty-seven-year-old drummer for a new wave band called Funk-Chanel sincerely what you want?"

Kristina was stacking Dayglo sunglasses onto a mirrored, revolving display stand.

"Probably not," answered Kristina, a bit reluctantly. "But he's not fifty-seven. He's fifty-six."

"Excuse me!" asked a teen girl, approaching Kristina. "But do you have any rainbow knick-knacks I can buy with my parents' money and be embarrassed about in a few years?"

It was a typical question and Kristina was tired of it.

"No," said Kristina, still stacking sunglasses. "Try the Unicorned Rainbow. In the *rich* area of the mall."

This girl should have known better than to walk into a store with a dimly lit back area with hundreds of second-hand, genital-shaped candles and to ever expect to find anything rainbow related.

"If you could choose *anyone* to date, who would it be?" Addy asked. "What would be your dream?"

"The assistant manager at the stereo store," said Kristina, without delay. "But he has Herpes Simplex 4. And wears leather shorts. And he once asked, 'Scope on anything that lights your fire, chick?'"

"Who else?" asked Addy.

Kristina turned to face her old friend. "Addy! Since when did we become so questioning? I thought that was *my* job."

Addy, a bit wounded, pinched out: "A lot has changed over these past few weeks for me."

"I can see that," self-righteoused Kristina. "I'm so sorry you've had to go through as much pain as you have with Roland. He made you look foolish. But you seemed to have grown the better for it. I guess we've all grown within that interior room where we do nothing but sleep, cook, watch soap operas and change our grades. Now my question to you is, *If you could date anyone, who would that be?*"

"Roland's been calling non stop, begging me to believe the contest wasn't his idea," said Addy. "But I don't know whether to believe him. I want to, but ..."

"How about the Chonger?" Kristina asked.

"I suppose it's a possibility," said Addy, after a little thought. "He can dance, at least. But he has American girlfriend now. And, to be honest, I'm turned off by his corduroy ripper wallet that contains nothing but a single, disintegrating rubber."

"There's only one other possibility."

"And who might that be?" Addy asked, already kind of knowing the answer.

"*Grimer.*"

"Grimer?!" questioned Addy. "No way! We're just *friends*. You know that, Kris!"

Kristina shot her an *Oh please!* look. It was comparable to her *Oh c'mon!* look ... but ever so much more *intricate.* She had hired an expensive private tutor to teach her.

"Ask him to Prom, Addy. *Please*. What could it hurt?"

"There's still a chance I'll be going with Roland," said Addy. "And besides, the Prom's pre-embarrassing cut-off date was yesterday! Worse comes to worse, I'll just attend my sister's wedding. And then cook up some Jiffy Pop and watch the neighborhood idiot, Cliff, slingshot rocks through clouds."

Addy was slipping back into her please-feel-sorry-for-me yummy state ... and it felt *good.*

194

"It's *never* too late," answered Kristina, not entirely convincingly.

Years ago, Kristina had asked someone out to the senior prom when she was only a freshman. The entire school had become well aware that it was *long* past the "date of embarrassment" to ever ask out your forty-five-year-old P.E. teacher.

He had said "yes" regardless, mistaking Kristina for a colleague asking him to chaperone the dance.

"Do you really think he likes me?" Addy asked.

"Are you kiddin'? Remember when he unicycled in full harlequin makeup? You think he was doin' that for any other reason than to impress you? Why else would he pick you up at the country club in a stolen miniature horse, only to be tackled by police officers on I-55 and then run off into the woods to escape? If you can't ask him to prom, then at least ask him to be your boyfriend. Hot fudge you waiting for already?"

Kristina, who was so very street wise, loved to drop a letter here and there, replacing it with a well-earned apostrophe, all Cabrini-Green like.

"You know, my sister said the same thing," Addy said. "But I'm only a sophomore!"

Her sister had actually said no such thing but that was okay. Addy liked to agree.

"And he's a senior. So he's *legit*. Do it," continued Kristina.

"If I do, you have to promise me to apply—"

"To become assistant manager at a store in the richer part of the mall," finished Kristina. "And to date someone closer to my own age. *Fine*. Promised. Now 'git.

Ya hear? No more sass, chile!"

That urban street wiseness again.

"Thanks, Kris," said Addy. She paused. "For *every-thing*."

As Addy made her way out of the store, a young teen passed her and approached Kristina.

"Yes?" Addy could hear Kristina ask.

"Do you have any rainbow-related knick-knacks I can buy with my parents' money and be embarrassed about in a few years?"

Addy grinned. She *really* did love this mall! What a special, *special* space! This monument to pre-fabricated festivity would certainly be around for as long as teens wanted to socialize in a consumerism-saturated, Disney-like environment, guarded by poorly-vetted middle-aged men barely earning minimum wage, run by vast corporations thousands of miles away.

Into the amazing future! And beyond!—

Uh oh!

Addy heard the large glass "penalty box" explode onto the first floor. There were screams. The frayed rope must have finally snapped. Addy could smell death.

Meanwhile, on the other side of town, Pribbenow was sitting in a diner booth at the Cherry Pit with Roland. They had a lot to talk about.

"Why would you do that?" asked Roland again, hurt. "And why wouldn't you tell me you were going to?"

"The ugly loafers testy-test? It was a funners, babe!" answered Pribbenow. "You don't like toying with Yoids? C'mon, we've *all* done it before!"

"I haven't," said Roland. He appeared genuinely sad.

"Nothing I say can convince Addy that it wasn't me. I genuinely thought it was an ugly shoe contest. I've been calling forever."

"What're you worrying about?" said Pribbenow. "You're gone in a few weeks anyway. It's off to Kenmont College for the both of us. The best mid-tier school in the country that tax-sheltered money can buy."

"I like her, okay?" said Roland. "She's different from the rest. Mysterious. Artsy. Or at least she claims she is. She ... says things that I wouldn't ever think about, not in a million years. Or even *understand*. But they sound like they could be interesting. And she looks ... *different*."

"She sure does," said Pribbenow.

"That's it," Roland said, snapping his fingers as if he just solved a complicated puzzle.

"What's it?" asked Pribbenow.

"It just hit me. Why you're acting like this. You *like* her. You have a crush on her but she's not interested in you, never has been. You're just *jealous*."

Pribbenow looked up from the huge cocaine mound in front of him. He had globules of white dust on his nostrils and a thin layer precariously balanced on his eyelashes. He looked exactly like a rabid snow owl out for a rare daytime flight.

"Absurd," Pribbenow said. "Of all the assumptions! She's a *tramp,* scamp! Nothing more, nothing less, Tess!"

Roland sucked back his own bump. "It's true and you *know* it!"

"All that I know," continued Pribbenow, "is that I love my friend and I want what's best for him. And that's for him to pull his head out of the muck of the South Lake."

"You're *something*," said Roland. "You've *always* wanted what I have! Whether you even want it or not! You're really ... *something*!"

It wasn't an expression so much as a failure to fill in a missing noun.

"I am something," grinned Pribbenow. "I am most indeed. *To us!* A victor mentality!"

Roland sighed. There was nothing that could be done with this guy. He was who he was. Always had been. Always would be. Not a bad guy. But not to be trusted. And a bit of evil in him. He would one day run his father's Savings and Loan banks. He'd be fine. Their friendship might end, but that was also fine.

The pumpernickel bread bowl was nearly filled to the brim with cocaine.

There was nowhere for these two to go.

The afternoon stretched before them.

They bumped on.

CHAPTER TWENTY

Dancing the Day Away!

Addy took a left into Hallway D and waited for the bell. It was time for yet another pep rally. She'd leave that to the students who needed to be pepped. She was doing just fine, thank you very much.

Addy made sure no one else was watching, and when the bell did finally ring, she slipped seamlessly into the Back World by way of a small hole beneath the school's payphone.

Grimer was in the Lair, just as always. Lucy was there, too, of course. As were Cass and Danielle.

Lucy was explaining to Cass why a sting from a Brazilian bullet ant was the most painful sting on Earth. "They only attack if they're attacked. So it's *deserved*!"

Danielle, not listening and wearing a Sisters of Mercy T-shirt, was frying up eggs on the new stove they'd recently installed, just next to the bisque-colored refrigerator and the Lucite-encased, wall-mounted, push-button telephone. She was singing the Enjoli perfume theme: "I can bring home the bacon, fry it up in a pan. And never, never, never let you *forget* you're a man ..."

The place was shaping up nicely. The horrible Christmas lights had long since been taken down, and Kristina had tastefully decorated the huge room with returned items from the Electric Salamander, including a few broken lava lamps and a huge halogen floor lamp that was returned after burning down a house. Beyond that there were posters, chairs, rugs and even a working fish tank.

It was like the interior of the *I Dream of Jeannie* bottle, without all of the obnoxious purple throw pillows.

The stolen soda machine from outside the gym now dispensed—instead of cans of Mello Yello—cans of V-8. It was a much healthier choice—the Republican-run USDA had just enthusiastically credited it with meeting the daily nutritional vegetable requirements for a nourishing child's sodium-laced lunch.

Grimer was on a new couch—this one taken from the nurse's office, where an overturned cardboard box now sat for all those who were sick—reading a borrowed library copy of *Diversional Activities for Those Who Live within Public High Schools*.

The grand painting Grimer had been working on for so long was finally finished, leaning against the wall, with a white cloth draped over it. No one had yet seen it.

"What's a-crackalackin'?" he burbled, almost impishly.

"Follow me," Addy replied, with just that most delicious amount of imperiousness.

"Why?" Grimer asked. He wasn't wearing pants. Only a jockstrap and a feather boa over a T-shirt covered in glass beakers stolen from the science lab.

"Just *follow*," she replied, leading the way out of the Lair and into an inner hallway.

Addy no longer needed a flashlight to find her away

around the Back World. Behind her, the *clank-clank-clank* of Grimer's shirt resounded and echoed. A muted cheer could be heard from the gymnasium, the backwash from the pep rally now taking place about the upcoming prom.

Throughout the back corridors Addy and Grimer traveled—these passages always reminded Addy of the narrow, dark alleyways in a movie she truly despised, *Blade Runner* (too dark, not enough pink, nowhere near enough angst, where were all the futuristic, preppy, robotic Richies?)—over galvanized pipes, under steel joists, across ropes and wood planks, higher and higher, to the point where even Grimer, who lived within the school his entire life, had no idea where they were headed.

The noise from the pep rally lessened; luke-warm applause that might as well have been coming from a distant reality.

It all had no bearing on Addy anymore. No longer bored by the intricacies of that other world, she could now fully concentrate on this one, the only world that mattered.

Grimer was breathing heavily. Addy, who had lost weight since discovering the Back World, had very little problem climbing higher and higher. Her strength only intensified.

"I've never been this high before," said Grimer, panting. "Why are you taking me here?"

Addy ignored the question and eventually stopped before a large, heavy door.

"Grimer. You *deserve* this."

She pushed open the door.

Grimer saw a long, dingy attic, paneled with wood floors, covered from top to bottom in thick dust. It seemed to stretch into forever.

This looked awful, too.

In the middle of the room sat a small, round table, lit by a lonely candelabra with many fancy candles, not one of which was genitally-shaped.

Addy took Grimer by the hand and led him over to a table, obviously stolen from one of the classrooms. On a wedding plate Addy had taken from her own home sat a cold mound of microwaved tater tots. Off to the side were the appetizers: multiple packets of Lik-M-Aid Fun Dips, in *all* the hot, new 1980s flavors: cherry, lime, wild apple, bone broth.

It looked awful.

"You did all this for me, Addy?"

"I did, yes."

"I can't tell you how much this means to me. I really can't."

"Because of your excitement-induced speech imped-iment?"

"No," said Grimer. "I just forget the word."

"We'll eat later," said Addy. "Come with me."

Through the cracks in the wood-splintered floor beneath them, Addy could hear and see the entire student body, some drifting off to sleep, some nodding their heads in time, as they sang along to what the pep band was playing, with the flutes leading the way: "I watched the needle take another man! Gone, gone, the damage done!!!"

Neil Young's "Needle and the Damage Done."

It was the perfect school "jam."

"Let's slow dance," said Addy, taking Grimer's hands in hers.

Addy could tell Grimer was nervous. He was sweating more than usual. A funk was emanating that Addy had not smelled since that hot, gassy stench of "arm curd" had grown beneath her cast in fourth grade, the one she'd poke with a curvy rubber pencil and sniff whenever she grew bored, which was often. Her teacher would later self-publish a children's book about it. The curd spoke in a British accent.

The two frolicked between the bissected lights beams, Grimer still not wearing pants, his glass beaker shirt clink-clankin' away. Addy looked at the candelabra and thought how easy it would be for her to tip it over and propel the school into a hellish inferno.

It would actually be kind of cool ... at least she would be remembered ...

"This is nice," said Grimer. "I never listened to this song before. It's very romantic."

"Can you promise me something?" Addy asked.

"*Anything.*"

"That when you leave this place in a month, you'll pursue your dream of the arts. To draw and paint. To go to art school. I'll join you in two years, when I myself graduate."

"Oh, I'm not going anywhere," said Grimer, matter-of-factly. "I'm staying right here. The money's too good. I also have grand plans for the Inner World."

"Meaning what?" asked Addy.

203

"Meaning I'd like to rent out space to graduating seniors who never want to leave high school. Condos."

The arts don't pay, her father had always told her. Addy shrugged. Fine with her. A few more years with the Grimer. There were worse things to look forward to. Very few but some. Or not. Addy was tired.

Trying to be helpful, Addy suggested: "You know, you could offer time-shares to weirdo kids from *other* schools. Make even *more* money."

Grimer wasn't listening. His mind was on other matters.

"Addy," he said, softly. "Addy, this may sound crazy but ..."

"But what?" asked Addy, curious. *Where could he possibly be going with this?*

"Banana down the upswing sloping on the bang bang hoof," Grimer said, almost shyly.

To Addy, it *did* sound crazy.

But who cared?

God, it was so pleasant to just dance with someone other than a giant yarn person! Even if he did happen to live inside the school and light his hair on fire and wear full harlequin makeup just for the attention.

Here, right before her, was a human being, a living and breathing creature, flesh and blood, a *real-life* creature with a non-yarn erection and who wasn't afraid of fire!

Grimer cleared his throat. This was harder in real life than in his fantasy world. Everything was so much easier in that world, minus all those floating imaginary creatures with translucent wings!

But real life, that was something else entirely …

"Addy," Grimer started hesitatingly. "I hate to admit this but …"

"But what?" asked Addy.

"I've never bagged a babe before."

"I know," said Addy, laughing.

A bit offended, Grimer asked, "How?"

"Anyone who's bagged a babe would never say 'bagged a babe.'"

Grimer would have to remember this. He cleared his throat and looked up to the dusty ceiling. Shyly, he asked: "Would you, um, go to prom with me?"

For a long while Addy said nothing. The pep band below launched into a brassy, upbeat version of Harry Chapin's "Cat's in the Cradle."

The most clichéd of all pep rally "pick-me-uppers."

"It's all too confusing," Addy finally answered.

"I understand," said Grimer, not understanding. "Now will you promise *me* something?" he went on. "Would you promise me that one day you will leave this place and follow your dreams? And we will both be happy, either with each other, or with someone else? Doing what we love most: producing useless art for an ever-increasingly commercialized world? And always remain friends? Will you promise me that?"

Addy nodded. She hugged Grimer even tighter, but still from a safe distance.

"I will," said Addy.

"Will what?" asked Grimer, not quite believing.

"Go to prom with you," said Addy.

"Oh, Addy!" yelled Grimer. "Oh, *oh* Addy! I always

dreamed of this! I will not let you down. I *promise* you that!"

"I know you won't," said Addy. "I really do, Grimer."

"In the meantime," he said, smiling as wide as Addy had ever seen, "we have some Richie business to take care of ... *do we not?*"

There was a tone in Grimer's voice that Addy had never heard before. She liked it. Assertive. Self-assured. Almost overly confident. Like the sound of her piano tutor's back in the fifth grade, the weirdo who began every session with: "Mother says there are rats in the rockery. We must kill them before they overrun us."

Addy grinned.

There was still, indeed, *business* to take care of.

A new song could be heard below from the pep band. This one was tuba-driven. It was called "I Need (At Least) Five Boys."

It sounded as if it was written especially for Addy and her current impossible situation! The only teen at this very moment who *truly* mattered!

And on they danced:

I need at least five boys ...
One to kiss my neck.
One to cook my dinner.
One to do the dishes.
One to make me laugh.
One to help with homework.
One to fight on my behalf.
One to sing, one to dance,
One for shopping, one for romance.

One for each finger, one for each toe ...
One to make the fire, one to just admire.
One to keep mom drunk, one who's just a hunk,
One who's normal ... and one who just ain't like
the rest,
I guess that would make for twenty boys,
Ten for each of my cheeks, ten for each of my
toes ....

CHAPTER TWENTY-ONE

What a Day, O, What a Day!

A few days later, Roland, as he did each and every weekday morning, drove his Karmann Ghia convertible—Gentile Gray—the 3.2 miles from his house to Northridge High's extensive campus.

And, as was typically the case, Roland was listening to a cassette mix he had put together himself called "Music 2 Drive 2 School 2 Feel Good 2." All of the 'twos' were represented, in a very modern fashion, numerically. It consisted of one song on repeat: "The Power of Love" by the great Huey Lewis of the News. Roland dug this song because it was uncomplicated and it didn't make his brain hurt with "lessons" or "meaning."

Roland was extremely proud of this mix. He would have to make another awesome mix tape real soon. Perhaps Bad Company's "Feel Like Makin' Love" played for ninety minutes straight, his all-time favorite make-out song.

That or AC/DC's "Highway to Hell."

Wait, what was this?

Did he just see right?

Roland slapped the Ghia's automatic stick into reverse (manual was only for the Blue Collars) and efficiently backed up the twenty or so feet to the school's high-tech LED sign, where he stopped.

It was right there, in futuristic white digital mall-arcade font:

ROLAND MCDOUGH DON'T GOT NO DOUGH!

What the?

Roland put the car into Drive and rocketed into the school's parking lot.

He exited the car (god, how he wished he owned a Lamborghini with doors that popped out *vertically*) and stormed into the school. Were people looking at him? And not in an affectionate manner? Were they aggressively *pointing* at him?

Where were all the Lessers with their argyle clothing and helmets when he needed them most? Or at all?

At home comparing physical imperfections?

"Babe," Roland heard.

It was Pribbenow. *Of course.*

"What?" Roland asked, distracted.

"Babe, you might want to go upstairs and check out the digital display in Doc Mulligan's office."

"Why?" Roland said, stopping.

"You might just want to take a look," pompoused Pribbenow, swiping an errant strand of hair from his forehead with a pinkie.

"Just tell me," said Roland.

Pribbenow giggled. "Officially, you're no longer a Richie, babe. Overnight you've become a Shit-Stained Flushy!"

"The digital board says that?" Roland asked. "The board actually says *that*?"

"As clear as Cristal," answered Pribbenow. When no one laughed, he said: "With an i. 'Cristal.' The *Champagne*."

Still no one laughed.

"It's *funny*," Pribbs insisted, showing them all his well-used copy of *You Might Be a Richie If ...* joke book. He opened to a dog-eared, well-worn page and pointed. People still weren't biting. He placed the book back into the interior pocket of his blue blazer. For later.

"It *really* is funny," he mumbled again.

But Roland wasn't having any of Pribbenow's top drawer, aristocratic humor. "You know what? You're a real floater, Pribbs. Get flushed!"

"Ouchy!" said Pribbenow, putting up a hand as if to block the incoming blow. "Messenger, babe. Just the *messenger*!"

"And did you read today's *Observer*?" asked Jill Standish, holding hands with Pribbenow.

"No," said Roland. He appeared pale, without color. Which was fine.

He had *never* read the school's newspaper. *Who had?*

"Not good," said Pribbenow, buffing his finger nails with an imaginary emery board, something he did whenever bringing up bad news or while having sex. It greatly helped soften the disappointment.

"Seems that your father earned his money the *hard* way and not by inheriting it. *New money*. Ain't good, babe."

The use of the word "ain't" was so deliciously south of the lake.

"Not true!" shouted Roland. He was infuriated.

"There's been money in my family for generations! My relatives were the first to mock the Pilgrims' obnoxious austerity!"

"Not according to Addy Stevenson," sing-sang Jill. "Her column in today's paper says that your father invented the thigh master. For *himself.* Two years ago."

Roland felt faint. Not positive faint. *Negative* faint. Like that time he had passed out after seeing a chef at a Benihana's chop off his own thumb while attempting to create an Onion Explosion. Addy's father later incorporated this event into an exceedingly unpopular commercial for a local dry-cleaner's.

"Better go find her, babe," ejaculated Pribbenow. "Before this shit stain becomes *permanent.*"

Roland stalked off toward the "Yoid Hall," a place where he knew a lot of Yoids liked to hang ... he had seen it himself during flex times.

"Do you know an Addy Stevenson?" he asked a passing Yoid.

The Yoid shook his head no. He was wearing a Rush concert T-shirt, a band Roland hated more than any other. Their complicated, syncopated beat and fantasy-based lyrics made his head and stomach hurt.

"You know Addy Stevenson?" he asked another passing Yoid, this one wearing a T-shirt with a decal of an apple on it, half eaten, next to a decal of a computer.

"Forget it," Roland said, before even waiting for an answer. He *hated* computers. Too clever by half. And half-eaten apples. Good luck to this fucking moron. He was like Benny from *L.A. Law,* but without the charm.

Roland rounded the corner.

211

"You looking for me?"

It was Addy.

There she stood, right before him.

Roland was just about to compliment Addy on her looks—she truly *had* made an impressive and full transformation—but he pinched himself as a reminder that he was still upset with her.

"Hurts!" he said in response.

"Excuse me?" asked Addy.

Roland ignored her question. He asked one of his own, one that actually mattered, one that wasn't so much as white noise: "What gives you the right to change the sign out front to something like *that*, Addy! I have sincere feelings for you. Open your Yoid heart to a gorgeous Richie, why don't you!"

"You know why, Roland! You're an ass."

"An *ass*?"

Roland was once or twice called an ass*hole* but this seemed a bit ... general.

"Why did you embarrass me like that? To have the nerve to invite me to such a contest?"

"I've left ten messages with your mother. I had nothing to do with it. *Honestly*, Addy! Your mom didn't tell you I called?"

"No," said Addy. "She only told me that someone from beyond the grave was calling to sell shoes."

Roland paused to process the discrepancy.

"It was Pribbenow. I promise you, Addy, it wasn't me. He's only jealous. The contest was his idea. He's competitive! If I like you, he has to then like you, too!"

"He likes me?" asked Addy. *Pribbenow? How was*

that even possible?

"He does," said Roland. "But I still want you to be my date to the prom!" he added quickly.

To Addy, it sounded like he actually meant it.

And then, as if attempting to close a sale, Roland said: "I wouldn't expect you to go with anyone else!"

Addy did not respond, merely turned and effortlessly slipped back into the Yoid scrum, leaving a frustrated Roland in her wake, screaming: "Wait! Addy! *Wait!*"

But then, noticing all of the Yoidy looks, Roland announced confidently, "Doesn't matter! Have to head over to the stables to comb out the miniature horses!"

This was a lie. Whinny was still fast asleep in a jail cell after the horrific drive home from the country club. She might remain asleep for a long, *long* time. Roland would just love to know who had kidnapped Whinny and run off into the woods to escape the police, leaving his championship mare all alone on the expressway to answer the tough questions.

Roland stepped forward one last time and yelled, "Adddddyyyyy!!!!!!"

Yoids turned to look.

Some whispered amongst themselves.

Roland stopped.

Wait. What was he doing? He didn't need this. Screw everyone!

He could so easily head back home and take a long, luxurious soak in his extra large hot tub filled to the brim with bubbling Diet Tab. Maybe he would even switch it out with Mr. Pibb, as it was more expensive. Afterwards, he would play a quick game of solo laser tag on his private course. He would pretend to be the heroic Bruce Willis, so brave and so capable of delivering a hilarious quip at just the right moment! Roland had already written down a list of barbed zingers on a cheat sheet to get himself started, a sidesplitting few having to do with fax machines.

"I'll see you at prom," he yelled after Addy. "There's no way you're not going. And I never *un*-invited you!"

A very loud sound could be heard.

It was coming from *outside* the school.

From *above*.

Roland walked outside the school and squinted up. There, just above him, circling, was an airplane. A small one. A banner advertisement was attached.

The banner read: *Addy Stevenson is 4 Real! ButT Roland is a F8ke!*

Students were beginning to exit the school, staring and pointing. Some were laughing. Some were even laughing *at* him.

It was hurtful.

The plane continued to circle. It now appeared that leaflets were being thrown from out of it—thousands, spread everywhere, papering the entire high school grounds and even into the suburban development beyond.

Eventually, one landed close enough for Roland to pick up.

He quickly scanned it.

On yellow paper it read:

101 Reasons Why Roland McDough Is An Ass!

Number 17: "Roland gets off on watching Spuds McKenzie conga dance with humans!"

Number 38: "Roland owns a Kangol jockstrap!"

Number 67: "Roland cried at the *Little House* episode when Pa exploded!"

A propaganda leaflet!

Just like those dropped over inner cities to attempt to turn the tide of the Drug War!

How in the hell had Addy known all this about him? Was she a witch? Even worse, a Democrat?

Roland couldn't imagine a more effective method in which to spread fake news and information. No one would ever improve on this.

Roland kneeled and put his head in his hands. This was all too much.

It was like filling out the Word Jumble in the Kids' Section of the Sunday *Tribune* but times one.

It was *way* beyond his comprehension.

Roland longed for the simplicity of a Huey Lewis song.

Meanwhile, back inside the school, Camilla, the short lead tumbler for the Lazers, was opening her locker when a bowling ball fell from above and knocked her unconsciousness. She potentially would now suffer a lifetime of brain damage.

It was hilarious, as is all violence involving unlikable characters.

Up on the third floor, at the very same moment, Jill

Standish was talking with Miss Andrews, her American History teacher.

"Jill, I have read over your final essay and it was ... very interesting."

"Thanks!" exclaimed Jill.

"But I never realized that the Civil War's outcome was determined by a breakdance battle."

"But …" started Jill. "I *didn't* write that. I would *never* write that. Seriously. I have no sense of humor. My friends tell me that all the time!"

"Sorry," said Miss Andrews, pointing to the paper she was holding. "But you did."

Seven more years. That was all for Miss Andrews. Seven more years and she'd be out of this hellhole and luxuriating down in Tampa at her one-bedroom time share. Three more years after that, she'd die from a massive heart attack while playing shuffleboard.

There was so much to look forward to ... but all of that was down the road. For now, however, it was time to flunk her least favorite student.

It would be an honor.

Meanwhile, in the classroom next door, Blaize, Dashiell, Magnus, Beff, Declan, Garth, Volbeck, Barron and Camilla and any other number of Richies were glancing down at the grades they had just received on their final Calculus test.

They had all flunked.

They were extremely stupid when it came to math but were they this *stupid? Not a single answer correct? Every answer just a smiley face with a question mark?*

It was almost as if all of their tests had been hacked

and their grades lowered by computer.

Throughout the school, Richies and Near Richies alike were having large objects—including paint cans—dropped onto their heads via elaborate booby traps. Their expensive clothing was being ruined beyond repair by squirts of dark ink mysteriously coming from the ceiling above. Their final grades were being lowered from comfortably mediocre to just plain horrendous.

It was almost as if the entire school building was haunted and had now somehow turned its angry attention against anyone who was even considered to not be a Yoid.

It was almost as if Addy and her Hang Gang were finally getting their revenge after years of being bullied.

Back in the Lair, Addy smiled.

She prayed that Grimer, up in the stolen plane, would somehow know how to land.

Foolishly, he had skipped over that last and most important chapter of the borrowed library book *How to Pilot a Stolen Beach Airplane!*

You only attack if you're attacked.

So it's deserved.

Boy was it deserved.

Addy thought:

Ain't it a panic?

CHAPTER TWENTY-TWO

Spring Into Spring

It was a week later and there was a bounce to Addy's step. At last. After fifteen years, she finally had *bounce*.

Down the school hallway she nearly floated. She had the keys to the kingdom and it felt wonderful.

"Hi, Addy!" declared a Punker, in passing.

Addy nodded, gave a slight grin. In the past she might have merely panicked and said something stupid, such as "Hi." But now she said nothing, which was infinitely more *Ramba*. She did her best to avoid looking too closely at the sickening "passion mark" on the Punker's lower neck.

"Hey!" said a football player, the only Sporty Type in the school lucky enough to have snagged the coveted #69 jersey. "Aces!"

Addy knew very few athletes and even less about their sporty slang. Not knowing what else to do, she gave a thumb's up.

"*Way to show them poozers*!" exclaimed a Smart Rebel, headed in the opposite direction. "Walk on!"

Addy didn't know what a *poozer* was but she winked at him. She *never* winked. It was harder to pull off than an eye flutter. She just might have to hire Kristina's facial-expression tutor to make it all work properly.

"Hi, Addy!" announced a Dead Head, wearing yellow Jam shorts with tie-dye suspenders, and a derby hat with a Jack of Diamonds stuck within it. He had sideburns that connected to form a peace sign.

Wow. He really looked like an asshole.

This was a strange, wondrous feeling.

Practically everyone at the school, regardless of their social position, was becoming aware that Addy was pulling off a spectacular feat that had never been before attempted in the history of Northridge High.

She was making a Richie look silly.

She was making them *all* look silly.

The digital chart hanging in the principal's office on the second floor confirmed as much.

Addy hadn't seen Roland in the school for days now. Or any of the other Richies. They had all made themselves scarce. Roland had called yet again last night and left message after message on Addy's machine ("please, please, *please* just come to prom with me! I'll make it up to you, *big* time!") but she hadn't called back.

It felt good to be in a position of power.

It was the real-world equivalent of a song by Natalie Merchant.

But what exactly did Roland *want*?

Addy continued walking through the hallways.

She didn't know.

Maybe she'd find out soon enough.

Addy, still on the slunky, funky move, didn't slow her pace until the sun began to finally set, well into the late afternoon, long past the ring of the final bell.

Addy loved this time of the day the most, almost

sleep-walking through the empty, flickering-lit school hallways.

The only other students now at school were the members of the Dungeons and Dragons club, but Addy knew that if she ever were to actually see any of these kids (people rarely did) they'd only roll six-sided dice to determine their next course of action.

Addy felt sorry for them. In the upcoming years, they'd have to deal with a scenario *way* scarier than the beasts and the creatures sprinkled throughout their fictional kingdoms: real-life college sorority beings.

Addy stopped before a trophy case that held more than three decades worth of championship trophies.

Where were all of these champions now? she wondered. *Happy? Dead? Married? In a recliner, at home, watching sitcoms, wishing they, too, could somehow legally adopt a harmless black midget child?*

And if these past champions weren't happy, how about all of the names that were not on the trophies?

How were *they* doing?

Addy hoped to one day look back and re-invent entire high school stories and adventures that she could tell to her barely-listening grandchildren. In these stories, she'd be popular and beautiful and definitely not the type of girl to have ever felt the need to stay at home on a Saturday night to dress up her hermit crabs as Cyndi Lauper.

Addy carried on, beginning one final loop around the hallways—she had fifteen minutes or so before she had to leave for home—and she found herself passing the school's multi-floor library. She took a quick glance inside. She noticed that just next to the stairwell, the same group of five students, from all different cliques, but all from the same racial and socioeconomic makeup, were *still* sitting within their tight circle, chatting about something or other that was completely meaningless.

It had been *months* now. Just talking and talking and talking and *talking*, or dancing on that stupid wood banister, or dry humping that hideous statue.

What could they possibly be talking about all this time?

Addy saw that the school's middle-aged janitor, Robbie, was also still in the library. He looked as if he just wanted to get home to his family.

Desperately.

Out of all of these characters, Addy thought, *This is the guy I emphasize with the most.*

Robbie the janitor looked up. He smiled. He walked quickly out of the library towards Addy.

He just needed an excuse—any excuse.

And he had just found one.

"Too much talk," sighed Robbie, holding a push broom. "My god, the talk."

"What are they saying?" asked Addy. "What have they been talking about for weeks?"

"At this point, I'm barely listening," said Robbie. He looked exhausted. "Besides, they have it all wrong anyway. It's all so simple."

"Yeah?"

"Yeah," said Robbie. "Be a good person. Make your own coffee. Be kind. Treat everyone with respect. Work hard. Work smart. Do what you want, how you want to do it. Live a good life."

He paused and smiled. He was missing a tooth and his hair was graying. "Be happy."

"Are *you* happy?"

Robbie considered this. "Happy *enough*. The people who say 'I can't complain' are usually the first to complain. I saw that once on a Ziggy cartoon."

"I just want to *show* all of them," said Addy, feeling very comfortable with this janitor. "Everyone who doesn't get me. I just want them to know that one day they'll be sorry they never knew me. I want to be a super success."

Robbie tamped down onto the hallway's floor with his broom, almost as if this were a stereotypical habit. He shook his head. "No. By the time you do achieve success, whatever the hell it is, your parents will be long dead and your classmates won't care anymore, not that they ever did to begin with. Most won't give a shit. They didn't from the start."

"It's that simple?"

"It is," Robbie answered, before glancing into the library.

He shrugged.

"Christ, they're calling me back," he said. "Why are you here, anyway? Aren't there better things to be doing? Isn't prom in a few days?"

Addy shrugged.

"You're not going?" Robbie asked.

"I've been asked by two guys," said Addy. "And I said yes to both of them. And there's even a third who likes me. So, I don't know."

"What's the theme this year anyway?" asked Robbie.

"*Don't you forget about me*," said Addy.

Robbie laughed. "Oh, they will. And so will *you*. And this'll all seem so stupid. Like a bad fever dream after eating a horrendous basket of nachos and melted cheese."

This happened to him, too!

They'd both have to avoid that particular concessions stand at Wrigley Field, beneath the bleachers and next to the stuffed cursed goat.

"Well, thanks," Addy said eventually. "You're wiser than you look."

"I know," said Robbie the janitor. "Ironic, right?"

The scene was almost like something out of a movie written by a man who never once had to work a janitorial job.

How did Robbie end up as a janitor, anyway?

Addy was curious.

How should Addy put this without offending him?

"How did you end up as a janitor anyway?" Addy asked, too lazy to even rewrite the question in her head.

"Never marry a woman with a forehead tattoo."

Jesus, was this a thing?!

"Okay," said Addy, a bit stunned.

Smiling, Robbie turned and walked back into the library. All five of the stereotypes seemed to be taking a break from chatting. The wrestler was aggressively making out with the former goth who was wearing a frilly little white girly-girl dress. She looked exactly like something out of Pribbenow father's X-rated Hummel collection.

Addy called after Robbie the janitor. "When you grow up, does your heart die?"

Robbie again laughed. "Maybe. Or maybe you're just too preoccupied with your mortgage payments. Go to prom. But do it *your way*."

He carried on.

Addy headed home.

CHAPTER TWENTY-THREE

Kissing the Pink

Addy was sitting in the backseat of the Tweedled-weeb, her father driving.

They were approaching the school, maybe five minutes out, when she started to weep.

"Hey," said her father, half-concerned, half thinking of fast-food slogans for the new ad campaign he was just assigned: to improve Jack in the Box's standing after that unfortunate E. Coli outbreak.

It was a plum gig.

He had already come up with one delightful gem: *"Fecal matter has no place here!"*

He was finally back on his creative game!

"Shouldn't *I* be the one crying?" he asked, jovially. "Spending all my hard-earned money on a wedding party that I'm now missing?"

"Princesses's marriage isn't going to work," stated Addy, flatly.

"No. Not at all."

Addy's father was wearing a rented tux over his putter-tattered cotton bathrobe.

"Then why are we going through with it?"

"Often you have no choice. But your sister will be just fine. She'll marry again, divorce, settle down, sort of, with a third husband. At that point I'll be dead. It'll all work out."

Addy said nothing. She didn't have to. She agreed.

"Thanks for letting me skip the wedding," she said eventually.

Her father shrugged. *Had Addy not just heard what he'd said about there being at least* two *more upcoming weddings?*

"What would you have done differently, daddy? If you could live your life over?"

"I've thought about this often," said her father, now driving with one knee. "To start, I probably wouldn't have left our first child home alone while your mother and I flew down to the Sandals Resort in Jamaica. At the time, we both found it cute. But four months was just too young for him to be left alone, according to the experts. Especially when house robbers are involved."

"I had an older brother?" Addy asked. She hadn't heard about this one, only about the six younger siblings, all of whom had died after being left alone as her parents partied.

Her father nodded, absent-mindedly, fully engaged.

"I guess another thing I wouldn't have done would be to travel on that cross-country trip with your aunt on the roof. She didn't deserve that—especially still being alive."

"Do you consider your life a success?"

"You know, if I can just affect one person in a positive way, I'd consider my life a success. Also, if I ever made enough dough to live at the very north tip of the lake."

It was a good talk! But now things took a turn for

the serious.

"Oh, daddy! *Daddy* ... this guy—this boy—he really is *so* beautiful," Addy burbled, dabbing at her eyes. "And the fact that he paid *any* attention to me, that doesn't happen often. In fact, it's *never* happened. It might never happen *again*!"

"Is he waiting there for you now? Or is it that other boy? The Gonorrhea?"

"The *Grimer*. He is, yes. But the Richie never *un*-asked me. And then there's that other cocaine-addled Richie who supposedly likes me too. I can't even imagine what to expect!"

They were now pulling up to the half-circular drive of the high school, filled with rented limousines and drivers who would have rather been anywhere else but here.

Couples in formal wear were milling around outside the school's entrance. They were connected via the Pinkie Hand Hold.

The Tweedledweeb came to a full stop. "God, I haven't been inside in so many years," her father said, appearing nostalgic. "Last time I was here, your sister had slept with the Spanish teacher."

He sighed dramatically.

"And she still received a D."

He paused. "Whatever happens tonight, Addy, I want you to know that I love you very much."

"And I love *you*, daddy." She leaned over to hug him.

"Haven't heard *that* in awhile."

"Please thank momma for this gold bracelet. It's so beautiful."

"She really does adore you. I snuck it out this morning when she was too drunk to care. She's still too drunk to care. But she really *does* love you."

Addy smiled. Her mother was indeed difficult and aloof and often incoherent from muscle relaxers. She was way too rash when it came to major decisions, especially financial; for instance, she was just about to flush a ton of money down the proverbial toilet by starting a Chonger's Crumbles store in the mall's foodcourt.

But it still occurred to Addy that—even beyond all this—it really *was* her mother who was the glue that held the entire family together.

The *Krazy* Glue ... but still ...

"Hug them *all* for me, daddy."

"I will," said her father. "Come back whenever. Have fun!"

He started to drive away but stopped the car within a few feet and leaned out the car's window:

"The world is a very *strange* place, Addy. A lot weirder than you could ever imagine. Nothing more than a vat of overflowing *insanity*!"

He pulled away again, this time for good.

Sweet, sweet daddy!

The most perfect of pre-prom speeches delivered at this, the most ideal of times ...

Addy felt very much alone, like an astronaut who hadn't yet exploded into space but who was about to explode into space and who wasn't all that prepared to explode into space. Or something similar. Addy wasn't big on rocketry.

Yet another rented limousine pulled up to the school's entrance and a group of energized students emerged, laughing. Addy caught a glimpse of the driver's expression. If it could talk, it might have said: *I never came to my own prom and now I have to drive these shitheads to theirs?*

When historians would one day write about this remarkable event—and Addy had no doubt that they would; it was sure to become an obligatory requirement for graduation within a generation—they would certainly start with Addy's homemade prom outfit.

It looked ... like nothing before created.

She ran down the items from her "dress checklist," starting from the top:

Bowler hat with attached aviation goggles ... *check.*

Shrinky Dink earrings in the shapes of the Deformed Creature from *Eraserhead* ... *check.*

An entire dress made out of American cheese wrappers that was coated pink with a gallon of Wite-Out liquid.

Was there anything more alternative?

Most "def" not.

Check!

Addy was back to her old self! There would be no more dressing "Richie" for her! *Never again!* She felt so much more comfortable: it was like slipping back into a soiled and filthy outfit long after having forgotten why she ever stopped wearing it to begin with ...

Addy walked toward the cool, neon-glazed, high-topped reality of kick-ass tubular synth-rockin' sounds and delicious phantasma-gaseous smells that represented PROM.

Whatever happens, happens! she thought.

She could hear, even from outside the school, the bassy thump-*thump*-thump and the giggles and the fake shrieks from the Passive-Aggressive Hug Club announcing that "No way, *your* outfit is *so much* better and it looks to be stain resistant!" and "Oh my god, you are *too* beautiful, you look like a professional hand model, don't give me *that* look!"

Addy would definitely have to join this club next year. She would start by practicing her passive-aggressive bullshit lines as soon the public pool opened for the summer in a few weeks. Who should she compliment first?

Perhaps Betty-Anne Robinson, the sixty-something feeb who worked the snack stand, on her frayed Minnie Mouse one-piece.

She took one last deep breath and prepared to open the door—but someone was already opening it for her.

Pribbenow!

He was grinning.

"Pribbenow," Addy heard herself announcing.

"The one, the only. What's kickin', little chicken? I'm so glad you came. Can't say I'm surprised. I knew you would. Because you ... *could.*"

That dreaded Richie rhyme!

Addy couldn't take her eyes off him. She thought: *He's repulsive ... but god is he rich! And he really isn't all that bad looking, if you ignore his silk kimono robe with a dragon on the back sucking on a snake's giant titty. And he does smell really nice ... like the aroma of a freshly opened LP album. It smells of ... possibilities.*

He was extending a hand in a most gentlemanly

manner, leading her into the school.

Deep inside, maybe Pribbenow wasn't so bad after all.

Perhaps he just needed a chance?

Perhaps she just needed to somehow reach his soft, gooey center?

"And here I was thinking you hated me all this time," replied Addy, all cool. "You've treated me so horribly. How could you possibly tell Roland that you *liked* me? Was it just because *he* liked me?"

"Sometimes you just can't help yourself, you know? Like walking past the woods and you smell a stink. But it's a *good* stink. There's always been something about you that I can't just put my finger on. I'm hoping tonight I can finally put my finger on it."

He smiled.

Addy asked: "Where's your girlfriend, Jill Standish? You never stopped going out with her, right?"

"No. But I could stop tonight."

"It was you who put together that horrible contest," declared Addy. It wasn't even a question.

"It was. All me. Roland's too stupid to have come up with such a fun idea."

"So where's Jill?"

"Seems that her parents weren't overly thrilled about her failing every single one of her subjects," said Pribbenow, shrugging.

Pribbenow had also flunked every single subject but his parents were a bit more "hands off" when it came to academics.

"Not that you need good grades for an M.R.S. degree

anyway," Pribbenow continued. "So where's Grimer? I saw on the digital board that he asked you to the dance."

"I have no interest in dating Grimer," said Addy. "I've moved on. I want ... *bigger* things to happen. Better."

"Nice," said Pribbenow.

"So what do you *want* exactly? To be my boyfriend? After all that you put me through?"

"A dance. That's all I ask," said Pribbenow, holding out his finger nails and receiving an imaginary manicure from a foreign worker, something he did whenever bringing up uncomfortable news. It was a very bad look ... but it was infinitely better than his fake imaginary pedicure.

Whatever happened, happened.

She felt carefree, untethered to any and all responsibilities.

"I have just one request. Could I have a dance with Roland first?" Addy asked.

"I don't see why not. As long as you come crawling—er, dancing back to me."

"Okay then," said Addy.

She ambled her way through the couples in the hallways, leaving Pribbenow by the front door. One girl, in a corduroy spinal correction neck brace (Ocean Pacific), had arrived stag. Addy assumed it to be a fellow student. Or maybe just a down-on-her-luck recent grad who was here for the free eats and company. The girl bent down for a drink at the water fountain but found that the huge brace prevented her from doing so.

It was surprisingly funny, as all sad fates involving

incapacitated people tended to be. It was almost as if the scene was written by a man who never once had a handicapped friend.

Addy strolled with purpose into the gymnasium. Thoughts from her amazing previous three months flickered before her mind's eye: parents forgetting the anniversary of her first period; Chonger "dance worming" his way from out of the cafeteria; Kristina's "I'M NOT A VIRGIN ANYMORE" button; Grimer being born in a bathroom stall during the 1966 Northridge High prom; Addy's aunt falling from the roof of her father's car while it was being driven through an Ohio car wash.

Now where was Roland?

The melodic sounds of the Simple Minds' "Don't You Forget About Me" resounded. Was there any song more romantic? Addy hoped to one day have this very song played at her wedding as she took her first dance.

That or Pink Floyd's "Goodbye Cruel World."

Hundreds of students, smiling, dancing. Richies, Preppies, Trendies, Attractives. Not a Loner or Shy One in sight. Most likely at home watching Monty Python or Albert Brooks movies on their pop-up VCR players.

Addy looked up to the gym's stage. There, playing their hearts out, were the REtroManiaCs, featuring one of Kristina's former boyfriends, Choad, who was now drumming while sitting down. He looked to be fast asleep. He was wearing lace gloves and a "severe suede" sweatband. The previous year he had stuck his index finger into a gearbox at the factory and received a $10,000 settlement that conveniently paid for his red and black electronic drum set with triangular pads.

The sound this band was producing was funky and urban, and Addy was happy that Choad had a new look.

It was so modern.

Someone approached Addy from behind. "Care to breakdance?" he asked.

Addy shook her head no. She was on the lookout for Roland. Besides, only pimps and foreigners broke dance.

She turned.

Oh my god.

It *was* a foreigner.

It was the Chonger.

Addy shrugged.

"Fine," said Chonger. "A *slow* dance it is." He took Addy gently into his arms and launched into a dance.

"I don't remember saying I *wanted* to dance."

Chonger laughed. "I don't remember either. But let's dance anyway, whatya say?"

"Wait. Did ... did you just talk without an accent? And use a lame Richie rhyme?"

"I did, yes."

"Where are you from, exactly? Not from the China continent?"

"D.C. area. Northern Virginia. And I'm Korean."

"How old are you?"

"Twenty-six."

"What are you doing here?"

"Free lodging. High school puss."

Addy nodded. Made sense. A twenty-something reinventing himself. *Perhaps the most American skill of them all.* Chonger had *nailed* it.

"You don't mind my mother stealing your Chonger's Crumbles idea? She did, you know. She's all set to open one inside the mall's food court."

"Nah!" said Chonger, pointing to his head. "*Plenty* of ideas! *So many*. Did I tell you yet about the store that only sells cardboard pieces for street breakdancing? I'm gonna call it Spinny's!"

Addy admired the guy, whoever the hell he was, con artist or not.

Her brother, Justin, would lose a good friend, true, but there was always *next* year's foreign transfer student to look forward to. She'd just have to remember to double-lock her bedroom door.

"I enjoyed staying with you," said Chonger, as the song finished. "Creeped the hell out by Yarnkin and your vicious mood swings. But you'll do okay."

"Where are you headed now?" she asked, genuinely interested.

"California. West Beverly High. That's where the early '90s will be at. As soon as I get a fade haircut and a neon leather windbreaker with a STOP sign on the back."

"Chonger? Is that even your real name?"

"Hell no. It's Eric."

"And you don't feel bad about playing a stereotype?"

"Jobs are hard to come by," said Eric, shrugging. "Trickle down. Thank your parents for me. They're nuttier than the stones in Reagan's kidneys but they're decent enough."

"I will," responded Addy.

Addy and Chonger hugged.

And then, just like that, Chonger was back in character and breakdancing away from Addy, screaming:

"Chonger just want to have fun! Chonger most extreme! Waxy to the maxy! Grab a bitchin' donut! Someone *kiss* the Chonger!"

Addy hoped some deceived girl would.

The song ended. A fresh one started. Another prom chestnut: "Love Will Tear Us Apart" by Joy Division.

The perfect romantic song for any young couple on this, the *greatest* night of their lives!

Addy felt a tap on her shoulder. *Please don't be the masturbating forty-something guy with the crutches who's wearing the pleated khakis,* she thought. She had caught a glimpse of him earlier, standing by the snack table, taking too great an interest in the pyramids of mini hot dogs. Last she saw him, he had been sky-toinkling himself atop the Sears tower.

She had no idea what he was dong here now. This guy was *everywhere.*

"Addy."

She knew who it was even before she turned.

It was Roland.

Of course!

"You hurt me," whispered Addy. She almost couldn't help herself. "Oh, how you *hurt* me."

"You hurt me back. Let's call it even, okay?"

"Well …"

"I *knew* you'd come. I never had any doubt."

"Really?"

"Well, not really. I was *hoping.* I'm so sorry for all that's happened, Addy."

Addy looked into his beautiful eyes. She saw a good-ness. A sweetness. Also, cocaine-induced dilated pupils.

"One dance?" asked Roland, extending a hand. "That's it? Just one *tiny* little dance? C'mon, I'm as harmless as a nun's habit!"

"At a forest orgy, right?" asked Addy.

"Huh?" asked Roland.

He was confused again. But it didn't matter.

Roland's yummy cologne was arriving a millisec-ond before its owner.

It was the difference between gold and silver.

"Okay," Addy said, almost hesitatingly. "One *quick* dance. And that's it!"

Roland took Addy in his strong arms and they began to dance.

The crowd around both Addy and Roland began to take notice.

They made a collective "oooooohhhhhhhhhhh" sound. The last time Addy had heard anything even close to this was in the finale to the *Mama's Family* episode when Mama died after falling into a huge pot of creamed corn.

Addy let Roland swirl her around and around, oh so leisurely. There was a single pink beam of concentrated light targeted—*dead-set, bullseye, smack dab in the exquisite center*—right on her face.

She prayed it didn't accentuate the nose bump. Or her slight mustache.

"I really do like you. I'll never again date anyone like you again. *Ever*! Not because I won't meet anyone like you ever again but because I probably just won't want to."

Addy nodded. He was speaking the truth. He always had been. Even if that truth was skewed and awful and dumb and mainstream. He really was not the brightest. But he almost *always* spoke the truth. Addy had to give him that. "I know," she said.

"And I know that you'll one day achieve all of your dreams and that they won't involve a lot of money. And that you'll make a difference on a small, boutiquey level. I just *know* it!"

"Thank you," said Addy. This dance wasn't so bad after all. "I appreciate you saying that. And I'm sorry for dropping the propaganda leaflets."

"Ah, that's okay," said Roland, shrugging. "My father is paying to have a batch dropped tomorrow over the school as a counter argument. Remember that story I told you about the famous fruit from Kashmir? Some are allergic but most aren't? And if you're allergic, you die? It's just that story printed on thousands of leaflets."

"And you came up with that? That's yours?"

"I did not. It was in the novelization to *Temple of Doom*. I think Short Round says it to a monkey. Anyway, Addy, I wanted to tell you ... because you *did* come tonight ... that I'd very much like to bestow upon you the greatest gift of all."

"And what that might be?" Addy asked, greatly fearing that it would be that *other* horrible story he once told, the one about plucking the dreams from her mind and throwing them high up into the air to form a beautiful constellation.

"Kissing the pink," explained Roland, slowly, carefully enunciating each word.

"Huh? What does that even mean?"

"*Kissing the pink.*"

"Meaning? You're planning on taking my virginity tonight?"

"No. That sounds like a nightmare. It means what we're doing *now*. This is what *this* is called. When you slow-dance at prom with only a pink spotlight shining right on you. With everyone watching."

Addy was confused. "I ... always thought that phrase meant something ... *different*."

"No," said Roland, patiently. "*This* is what it means. If a girl is lucky—I mean, really and *truly* lucky—such an event occurs only once in a lifetime. It's now happening to you. And to *me*. I consider myself lucky. *So, so lucky!* Thank you, Addy! I'm leaving for college in a few months, a school that'll accept just about anyone willing to pay in full. It's the only school whose mascot has an errection. When I get there, I promise to write you one time and then never again."

So this is what Kissing the Pink means! thought Addy.

She would have to add this phrase to her word and phrase journal. She'd then safely lock it into her Memory Trunk, the one stolen from the elderly neighbor with Alzheimer's. She would never have to add another word or phrase, which made her very happy. One day her daughter might stumble upon the trunk—say, in 2021—and cry out with a joy that was rarely seen amongst humanity.

She would no doubt be incredibly confused when it came to her mother's intense relationship with a giant yarn creature, but that was okay.

A little bit of mystery in life is good.

Addy envied her future daughter.

Around and around they twirled. And around and around they *whirled*. Swirling and whirling and twirling and hurling.

It seemed to last forever.

"So what does your father do to make $100,000 a year?" asked Addy.

"I wondered the same thing! I recently asked. He's facilitating the sale of arms to Iran to fund the Contras in Nicaragua while at the same time negotiating the release of several U.S. hostages. It's really all for the greater good."

Addy nodded. She hated Prom small talk.

But the delicious warm beam of the pink spotlight felt so good. Until it eventually dissipated. The song was over.

With the focused, bright light no longer shining in her eyes, Addy could again see all around her. Hundreds of students, smiling, applauding politely.

It was a nice feeling.

Roland kissed Addy gently on the cheek.

In return, he whispered: "Thank you again, Addy. By the way, Pribbenow is here tonight, too. I do know that he likes you. Take good care."

"I know," said Addy. "His dance is next."

Roland grinned. He was genuinely happy for her.

"But wait," said Addy.

"Yes?"

"This is for you," she said, handing over a button.

"For your white Izod. It's the type of button you're looking for. Wear it well."

He palmed it like a priceless jewel. "Thank you, Addy. I most certainly will." He placed it directly on his shirt, forgetting that it wasn't the white Izod he was wearing, nor was it the type of button one could just stick on. It fell to the ground. He grinned. He kneeled to pick it up. He really wasn't the brightest.

That was okay.

Roland stood off to the side with a smile and began a slow clap.

He carried on for a few seconds like this.

Then, seeing no one else joining in, he disappeared into the crowd, and was swallowed whole.

Addy was glad she had met him. But if she never saw him again, that'd be okay, too.

"Addy," Addy heard.

She knew who it was even before she turned.

"Ready?" Pribbenow asked.

"Yes," said Addy.

"Just one solitary dance. And then ... perhaps we can go to the football field. I want to express my love to you in a very *special* way."

"Excuse me?"

"Like I just mumbled because I desperately want to sleep with you: I want to *express* my love to you in a very *special* way."

Addy thought about this.

Whatever happened, happened.

"Could we go up to the stage first? To show everyone that we're now—you know—*together*?"

241

"Marvelous idea. I have something quite important to tell the entire school anyway. And I hope Grimer's listening. The smelly freak deserves to hear this, too."

Two lines of students automatically formed to the right and left of them, bookending their way up to the stage. Pribbenow cinched his kimono ever tighter. He was the first to climb up; he then helped Addy on to the stage. He grabbed a microphone from the lead singer of the RetroManiaCs.

Strong and proud, in a very masculine voice, Pribbenow announced, "*Ahem*! Attention, everyone! Thank you! These past few weeks have been real tough, not just for the Richies. But for *everyone* in this school. So I'm now hoping that we have proved, Addy and me"—he looked over to Addy. Was it Addy and *I*? Addy smiled but said nothing—"um, Addy and *moi*, that if *we* can come together, well, then *anyone* can come together!"

Pribbenow held Addy's arm up in a show of unity.

Two champions displaying what love truly looked like, regardless of the caste system!

A smattering of applause.

Is this really happening? Addy thought.

It was.

"Ladies and gentlemen. I have something to say and I want you to listen closely. The famous fruit of Kashmir is picked just once a year in a remote region above the Ishtar valley. These fruits are most beautiful and rare…"

Jesus in Dallas!, thought Addy. *Yet another guy plagiarizing the novelization to* Temple of Doom?!

No matter.

Addy stepped to the side, away from Pribbenow.

242

And then down off the stage.

"Um …" said Pribbenow into the mic. "Hang on a sec."

Off mic, hand blocking what he was saying, he hissed: "*Addy*! Where do you think you're going? I'm not done with my speech. And then we can head to the football field!" Spittle flew.

Addy noticed that Choad, the fifty-six-year-old drummer, was no longer asleep but fully alert to the current situation.

Or semi-alert. He launched into an electronic drum roll. It sounded terrible.

Addy said nothing. She continued walking away from the stage.

"I said, Where in the hell are you *going*?" Pribbenow whispered louder, not caring that the entire school could now hear.

"Eat dirt. Shit twice and die."

She also did not care if the entire school heard her.

Addy continued on.

And then, almost as an afterthought, she said, loudly enough for everyone to hear: "Kiss my Astro-Turf!"

Behind her, Addy could clearly hear the bucket dropping from the rafters above.

It was filled to the very brim with gallons of exceedingly thick chocolate shake.

A noise resounded. Addy could only compare it to a bucket hitting a human head but without the wacky sound effect of a slide whistle.

Like Camilla and the bowling ball, Pribbenow would now potentially suffer brain damage. It was almost as if the scene were written by a man who never experienced real-life tragedy first hand.

Regardless, it was hilarious, as all violence that involved criminals and unlikable people tended to be.

The ineffective drum roll stopped, followed by the crash of an electronic cymbal. That too sounded awful.

Enjoy, Pribbs. Have as much chocolate shake as you wish. Whatever you're comfortable with body wise! Your choice ...

A kind of magic happened. An implosion of time and space. Addy had never heard such sustained applause. Screams of joy, mixed with Pribbenow's screams of pain. She rode it out like a powerful wave, straight through the gym doors.

Addy passed the principal Dr. Mulligan who—if he ever realized that it was Grimer taking a shit each evening on his office chair and not the raccoon who lived in the marching band shed—would no doubt have *not* been clapping.

Out in the hallway, Addy quickly posed for the prom photographer—alone. Her smile was not faked.

By the time Addy entered the school's library, the sounds of the prom had disappeared behind her. Instead, she could now make out the annoying five characters so clearly—the stereotypical amorphously-sexual brain, the bloated-before-his-time quasi-athlete, the glum dandruff artist who wasn't quite "on the norm spectrum," the eater of warm sushi, and the suburban faux criminal—each of whom was talking, talking, *talking*. They seemed blissfully unaware that prom was taking place just a few hundred yards away from where they now sat complaining. Addy had a pretty good idea that they'd still be at it during next year's prom, too.

And possibly forever after.

Addy entered into the Back World. Her eyes, more out of habit than anything else, opened wide to take in all of the darkness.

But she quickly realized this wasn't necessary. The inner hallway was lit with tiny Fuchsia round-paper lanterns hanging from the low ceiling. It spread into the distance like a runway guiding planes for takeoff.

The within the within.

Worlds within worlds.

When Addy at last entered the Lair, it was like walking into a dreamscape, albeit one with a barely working toilet. Fuchsia round-paper lanterns, larger than the ones in the hallway, swung from the ceiling. The smell of something most delicious was cooking on the stove. A banner was hung across the entire cavernous room. On one side it read: *Addy Stevenson is 4 Real! But Roland is a F8ke!*

And on the other:

TWO MORE YEARS!!! BRING IT ON!!!!!

The "Hang Gang" was all here: Lucy, Cass, Kristina, Danielle, all lined in a row.

Addy warmly hugged each friend as she passed.

Was this what heaven was like? Walking down a long line, not making small talk, just hugging anyone who ever understood you?

If it wasn't, Addy wished it could be.

She walked over to Grimer, who was standing by a lever that had unleashed the bucket on Roland's head.

This strange, fetid creature asked: "How goes it, Addy. Does it good go?"

He had done it one last time: reversed the order of a clichéd greeting in order to make it sound fresher and more Ramba—wait.

Make that more Alterna!

Grimer yanked on the lever one final time.

They could hear Pibbenow's distant, plaintiff cries echo into the Back World: "Oh god! It burns! Why am I not leaving the stage?! I can't feel my legs! My spine!"

God knows what had just fallen on Pribbenow this go round.

Grimer turned to face an easel with a cloth over it.

It was the painting he had been working on for so long.

"Addy," he said. "For the past two months, I have been trying to perfect my magnum opus. You taught me that word."

Addy smiled.

Grimer went on: "And I would love to unveil it for you tonight. If you'd allow me."

Addy blushed. She nodded.

"Good. Addy, I made *this* for you."

He sounded almost shy.

Grimer lifted the white cloth to reveal a painting.

Addy began to cry.

The painting was of Addy. Nude. Spread-eagled on a couch, attempting to solve a Rubik's cube. Her tongue was out, signifying a deep concentration.

"Of course, I took some liberties. As to what you *really* look like nude. I hope I captured it accurately."

He adjusted his hat, which in reality was just a round globe from social studies that had been raggedly severed in half.

"Looks ... *accurate* to me," said Addy, wiping her eyes. It was the most terrifying thing she'd ever seen.

"I just wanted to express my love for you," said Grimer, handing over the painting.

"It'll look ... wonderful over my bed," lied Addy. She had to admit: this guy really *had* captured her vagina.

With that said, she'd have to find an industrial shredder, and fast.

If anything was going to hang above her bed, it would be a framed prom photo of her happily posing alone for prom.

"I'm so happy you love it!" Grimer announced, proud and a bit relieved. "One more thing: I have some incredible news!"

The Hang Gang leaned forward.

"I shall be attending the Chicago Art Institute this fall! I've decided to leave Northridge High after all! I have decided, after much careful consideration, to become ... an art student!"

"Grimer! That's astonishing! I can't believe you got in!"

"I didn't. I'll be living *within* the walls of the Chicago Art Institute. Regardless, I shall be moving on!"

He grinned and, just as he did whenever super-duper excited, emitted a smoky musk from a few secret glands.

"And I have some exciting news, too," said Kristina, just as excited. Everyone looked to her. "I got the assistant managerial job at the Unicorned Rainbow! I start tomorrow!"

Addy saw that Kristina was no longer wearing her hilarious "Obviously I've Made a Serious Vocational Error!" button. Instead, she was now wearing the reversible PRUDE/SLUT button, thankfully with the PRUDE side out.

"*And* ... I have a new boyfriend. One who is more age appropriate!"

Standing next to her was the forty-something, on his crutches, wearing his thin, pleated khaki work slacks.

So that's why he was here! There's someone for everyone, thought Addy. At least he was no longer mumbling "Tired."

Lucy, just off to the side, glanced longingly at Addy and thought: *The Queen in her colony.* She pressed the boom box. The Smiths launched into their ode to all things miserable and self-loathing: "Please, Please, Please, Let Me Get What I Want ... Or I'm Gonna Have to Write Another Whiny Song."

Addy crouched down into a kneeling and useless Shakespearean position, with one arm draped across her knee. She reached over for Grimer's hand. "May I have your hand in this dance, Grimes? To have and to hold? To mostly hold? And if the light is right, to *kiss*?"

Addy had long had a feverish crush on the Smith's lead singer but, last she heard, Morrissey—or "The Mozz-oleum" as he was called by the fawning British music press—was already seriously involved with a very special, beautiful adult female.

Sigh.

Cass the Ass turned off the overhead lights and

mumbled, "fuck'n A," which would become next year's most popular slang term. She had heard it the previous week from her older brother's friend after he had returned, bruised and super angry, from therapeutic wilderness camp.

Kristina flicked on the disco ball she had taken from the Returns Box at the Electric Salamander. Why anyone would ever return such a glorious object, even if it was broken and only throwing off a few beams of light that made everyone nauseated—*and not good nauseated*— was beyond Kristina.

It was magic.

Danielle, in charge of the track-lighting, lowered the light's intensity, pink-cocooning them all into a warm hive-like embrace. Her biggest dream was to one day provide the tour lighting for Siouxsie and the Banshees. If that didn't work out—as not all goth dreams always did—she would become a veterinarian who smoked.

Addy and the Grimer launched into a slow dance.

"What's your real name, Grimer?" Addy whispered into Grimer's Attached ear.

"Teddy. But I am, and always shall remain, *The Grimer.*"

Around and around they twirled, and around and around they whirled. Swirling and whirling and twirling and hurling.

Grimer's unique, overpowering, swampy, acrid smell no longer seemed to bother Addy. Neither did the fact that his hair was on fire. Neither did the fact that he was now suffering a terrible limp from the plane crash the other day. She pulled him even closer.

Let the others have their prom. The Rich Richies and the Well-Heeled Flushies and the Casherios would never truly be "Ramba."

Addy now reached out to her friends, and they all stepped forward, and they all became one with each other in the dance.

This prom was theirs and theirs alone.

They'd be together over the course of the next year and the year after that.

After that, who knew?

But for now, they all belonged to each other.

As for you, listener ... you see them as you want to see them, in the simplest terms, in the most convenient definitions ...

Passable in Pink!

Each one of them a shut-in who loves insects.

Passable in Pink!

Each one a strange boy who raised himself within the confines of a school.

Passable in Pink ....

Each one a teen who looks decades older and who works as an assistant manager selling mall tchotchkes.

Passable in Pink ....

And a faux goth who plays Prince songs on the sousaphone in the marching band.

Passable in Pink ...

And a girl with a nest of candy-apple red curls whose self-pity has long floated away.

Addy closed her deep-brown eyes, leaned towards a kiss that was more than due—in fact, very much *overdue*—and danced on.

HOW TO

BreakDance

LIKE U MEAN IT!

**<u>Everybody</u> wants to but not every one can!
Now even YOU can, in the comfort of
<u>your own living room!</u>**

- *"Buddha" Twizzles!*
- *Head Slides!*
- *Wobbles!*
- *Jack Hammers!*
- *Head Spins!*
- *The Shakes!*
- *The Pelvic Slithers!*

You've seen and watched in wonder as professional and urban dancers have spun their slinky way right into your suburban heart. Now you can also dance just like those who live in the cities! 45 minutes taught to you by the lead star of Slippin' into Dat Groove Stream, Renoldo "Slappy-Pang" Martinez!

**Put Your Best Foot Forward! And then Back!
Now spiN! <u>It Is Remarkable!</u>**

45 MINUTES

of head-spinning, magical dancing wonder! On VHS and Beta!

Send check or money order for $14.95 to PO Box 29191, Chicago IL 60007